POOR BOYS CHRISTMAS

AND THE GREATEST GIFT

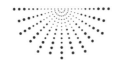

KATHLEEN BALL

This set is dedicated to everyone who encouraged me to write Poor Boy's story. He is a much loved character and he did indeed need his own book. Also to Sheri McGathy for her amazing covers and to Kay Springsteen Tate for her life saving editing. And as always to my loves Bruce, Steven, Colt and Clara because I love you.

FREE DOWNLOAD

Love Before Midnight
By Kathleen Ball

Get you free copy of "Love Before Midnight"
When you sign up for the author's VIP mailing list

Get Started Here

POOR BOYS CHRISTMAS

CHAPTER ONE

*G*unshots blasted from outside the stagecoach. Adrenaline filled Poor Boy Hastings as he drew his gun and lifted the window covering. The glare of the Texas sun poured through the window into the dimly lit coach, momentarily blinding Poor Boy. He squinted against the glare and waited for his eyes to adjust. By the time he saw what was going on, he realized he didn't have a shot. Two men were on horseback kicking up a good bit of dust while the Sheriff of Asherville, Shane O'Conner, was in pursuit.

The stagecoach jolted to a stop, and Poor Boy pushed the door open and jumped out. Quickly, he looked around and saw a saddled horse from his friend, Cinders' ranch. He raced to it and mounted in one smooth move. Then he turned the horse and rode hell bent in the direction he'd seen Shane go.

Cinders had been right, they needed a deputy. Spurring the horse on, Poor Boy gained on Shane. The sheriff didn't seem surprised to see him. He just nodded and urged his horse to run faster. It was no time at all before they had gained on the two bandits. Ragged and filthy bandanas covered the lower half of the outlaws' faces. One of them lifted his gun and pointed it at Poor Boy and the sheriff.

Poor Boy ducked a few times to avoid getting hit. One of the sheriff's bullets rang true and the larger of the outlaws fell to the ground. The smaller one instantly halted and dropped his gun.

He raised his hands. "Don't shoot!" The bandit jumped off his horse and sprinted to the downed man.

Shane vaulted off his horse and gathered the outlaws' guns. The smaller outlaw's hat slid back and fell off. A mass of pecan-colored curls tumbled down and settled about a set of slim shoulders. She pulled her bandana from her face and laid her head on the bigger outlaw's chest.

Shane exchanged astonished glances with Poor Boy, whose heart stuttered in his chest. The outlaw was a girl?

"Oh, Pa! I knew this would come to a bad end!" She looked up and glared at both Shane and Poor Boy. "You killed him! You murdered him in cold blood!"

Shane took a step forward. "Miss, listen. Shooting back at someone shooting at you is not murder. Maybe your decision to rob the bank is what led to his demise."

She gave Shane a hard stare before she lifted her pa's head and laid it on her lap. Tears rolled down her face as she stroked the dead man's hair.

Shane approached her with his gun still drawn. "You're under arrest. Poor Boy, grab the rope from my saddlebag and tie her hands."

Poor Boy complied and got the rope, but as he approached the grieving girl, he hesitated. What kind of father brought his daughter to a bank robbery? He sighed. He didn't know a thing about fathers. He had never known his father. He bent on one knee in front of the girl. "Put your hands out."

She tilted her head up and gazed at him with big blue

eyes. Her curly brown hair blew and twisted in the breeze. Resignation filled her eyes as she shrugged. With great care she laid her father's head upon the ground and put her hands out in front of her for him to tie.

He tried to be gentle, but tying someone up was not a gentle thing. Grasping her arm, he helped her to stand and then led her to his horse. Shane took hold of her arm while Poor Boy got on the borrowed horse. Reaching down he hauled the prisoner up in front of him.

"I can ride my own horse!"

"Should I send someone to help with the body?" Poor Boy asked, ignoring her.

"No, I've got him." Shane lifted the body and laid it over the back of the girl's horse. "You go on and get her into a cell. I'll be in town shortly. And Poor Boy, It's damn good to have you back home."

He gave Shane a nod before turning the horse and heading for town. The girl had tensed her body and sat as straight and as far away from him as possible. She shivered. She must be freezing. After all, it was December. It got cold in Texas in the winter. Not as nearly as cold as in New York where he'd been attending school, but cold enough. She didn't even have a coat on. Her hands looked red and chapped. She smelled nice, almost like lavender.

It wasn't how he'd expected his first day back to be. He'd been away a little over five years now. When he was younger, he had expected to come back to Asherville to live with his friend Eats. But Eats had died two years ago, and Poor Boy'd wanted to come back then with everything in him, but a lady in town, Edith Mathers, had insisted he finish his education before returning.

He hadn't had a choice back then. Now he had a job and he was sure he'd find a place to live. He might not have relatives still alive, but he had good friends. The best people he knew lived in Asherville.

He made quite the stir when he rode in on his borrowed ride with a prisoner in his arms. People first gawked and then greeted him. His heart filled with each greeting. There were a number of people he didn't know but town growth was a good thing.

A cowboy named Rollo came forward and grabbed the horse's bridle. "Hey, kid, good to have you back. I see you met my horse, Smart One." Rollo reached up and took the prisoner into his arms and then set her standing on the boardwalk in front of the jailhouse. "Did she rob the bank?"

Poor Boy got down from the horse. "Her and her pa, I guess. Her pa is dead. Shane is bringing him in."

Rollo instantly handed off the prisoner and then mounted Smart One. "I'll go meet him and make sure everything is fine. Darn good to have you back, kid."

Poor Boy opened the door to the sheriff's office and pulled the girl in with him. "Might as well tell me your name." He escorted her across the office and opened the door to one of the cells. He gently pushed her inside and closed the door. "Put your hands through the bars and I'll untie them."

She did as he bade. "I don't talk to the law. Not ever, no how. Torture me if you must but my lips are sealed."

He had to keep himself from laughing at her bravado. "Makes no never mind to me. I'll just call you Corny."

"Corny? What kind of name is that?"

"It's short for Cornelius. Corny, yes it suits you. Now, Corny, why rob the bank? I already know that the dead man is your father." His cockiness withered as tears poured down her face.

"I want him to have a proper burial."

He nodded, but he knew all a bank robber would get was

a hole in the ground without any words being said by a preacher. "The sheriff should be here soon." He turned from her and checked the coffee pot. Pleased to find it full, he poured himself a cup. A curl of steam rose from the cup, and he realized it would be better served to her. After all, she didn't have a coat.

MOLLY MCDONAGH ACCEPTED the tin cup filled with coffee from the man called Poor Boy. He appeared neither poor nor a boy. How strange. He was a man, a tall man with deep brown eyes and dark mud-colored hair. His certainly didn't have the shoulders of a boy. In fact, they were nice and broad. His clothes were a better quality than hers. Poor Boy indeed.

She wrapped her hands around the hot cup to warm them. Heck, he even had a coat on. What did she care anyway? Her pa was dead. Shot dead by that other man. Tears filled her eyes yet again. Would they have a trial or would they hang her right away? Right away would probably be preferable than waiting and wondering.

It wasn't as though she'd have anyone to mourn her. She was the last of her line. The last Mean McDonagh alive. She was as mean and as bad as they came. The irony of the name almost made her smile. With one mistaken allegation, her family had become outlaws. Live by the gun, die by the gun. Except that wasn't how they'd meant to live.

The sound of the door opening pulled her out of her musings.

A woman in a fine cloak with graying dark hair all wound into a tight bun came hurrying through the door, making a beeline for Poor Boy. She wrapped her arms around him so tight Molly thought he'd choke.

"Oh, my let me look at you!" the woman cried. "You're so tall and handsome. Oh my, the girls will just be over the moon to have you in town. You'll be so popular at the Christmas gathering. I'm so glad you're home. I kept Eats' restaurant going for you." She stepped back and smiled at him. "I can't believe you're here."

"It's good to be home. And yes, I've grown in the last five years. You never mentioned Eats' Place in any of your letters. I can't believe you kept it going."

"I hired a nice man, Aaron Pike, and his sister Ann Marie to run the place. Oh, you'll just love Ann Marie. She'll make some lucky guy a most wonderful wife."

Poor Boy's face turned red. "Let's not get ahead of ourselves, Mrs. Mathers."

"Oh, posh. It's Edith to you, my dear boy." She turned her head in Molly's direction , and her mouth dropped open, shock registering in her eyes.. "A girl? What is the world is a girl doing robbing banks?" Her lips formed a thin straight line and she shook her head. "The faster we get her type out of town the better."

Poor Boy's eyes widened as he gazed at Molly over Edith's head. "It's not for me to say. I'm just the deputy."

"What? Who said you could be a deputy? That's a dangerous job. You could get hurt or killed by someone like her!" She pointed a bony finger at Molly.

Molly took a step back. Edith Mathers was obviously not a woman to tangle with. She was nothing more than an uppity old hag. Molly turned her back to them. There wasn't much to see except the wall and the cot. The cot looked wretched with numerous stains on it. A bucket sat on the ground next to it. Her face heated as she guessed its purpose. The wall had names carved into it. Stupid criminals if they had something to carve with why didn't they just escape? Then again, she wasn't totally surprised. While on the run

8

with her pa, she'd encountered all types of not-too-smart outlaws. Now that she was caught, she probably fit into that category.

Hopelessness ran through her. She'd just turned seventeen, and it didn't look as though she'd see eighteen. She couldn't even admit it would be a waste. Her future would have been bleak indeed without her pa.

When she heard the door open and close again, she glanced over her shoulder. The old hag had left. *Good.* She drank down the coffee and then clanged the cup against every bar one by one in a sweeping motion in one direction and then again in the opposite direction making a loud, disturbing noise.

The startled expression on the deputy's face gave her a wicked sense of satisfaction. Perhaps she shouldn't feel so defeated yet. While there was a breath in her, there was life. She'd held on to her life so dearly before, why give up now?

"Hey, so about my name, how did you guess? My name is Corny Cornelius. I hail from Kansas. God's own choice place. Now I'm in hell, I'm in Texas. Anything else you wanted to know?" She shouted above the noise she was making.

He whipped his head around and stared at her before bestowing her with a heart-stopping smile. "No, that should do it for now."

———

THE CHALLENGE in her eyes intrigued him. She wasn't going to be the biddable prisoner after all. "Well, Corny Cornelius, it's nice to meet you. I wish it was under better circumstances, but we can't always choose what happens to us. Sheriff O'Connor should be here soon, and I'm sure he'll know what to do with you. It's my first day on the job."

Her eyebrow cocked. "I did notice the welcoming party you received. It might as well have been a darn parade. Why do they call you Poor Boy? Is it meant as a joke? You're neither a boy nor poor." She went back to hitting the bars with her cup.

He stalked over and grabbed the cup from her. "I think there's a rule about that."

"About what? Making music?" She folded her arms in front of her and subjected him to a saucy stare as though waiting for an answer.

He narrowed his eyes. She was baiting him. "Well now, if you were a man, I'd have cause to haul off and beat you. I'll ask the sheriff if the same goes for females." He pretended to cough to cover his laugh at the horror in her eyes. *Take that Corny Cornelius.*

"I'm sure females are to be handled with the utmost care. I mean not handled. Of course, I wouldn't want you to *handle* me at all. I mean—"

He roared in laughter. There was no help for it. The more he laughed the more pursed her lips became. "You know something, Corny? I think I like you after all."

"Good, because she'll be in your charge, Poor Boy," Sheriff O'Connor said as he came through the door. He set his hat on his desk and gave Poor Boy a bear of a hug. "Damn, it's good to see you! Wait until Cecily gets ahold of you. She's been so excited since word came you were coming home."

A shrill whistle came from inside the cell. "Is everyone in town related to you, *Poor Boy?*"

"I don't have a family."

"Sure you do! Heck, half the town lays claim to you. That's all everyone's been talking about for the last few months. That and the weather. Sure is starting to get cold out there. You never know what type of Christmas we'll have. Some years it's nice and warm and other times it's so cold your toes curl." Shane poured himself a cup of coffee and sat behind his desk.

Warmth rose from Poor Boy's neck and flooded his cheeks.

"So, your name is Corny?" Shane asked changing the subject.

She turned a bright shade of red. "Why yes, Corny Cornelius."

"It that right? If you're looking for an outlaw name that one is already taken. His wanted poster is on the wall over there." Shane pointed to a spot on the wall next to the door.

"It is?" She turned and glared at Poor Boy.

He smiled innocently at her. "She wouldn't give her name so I suggested it was Corny."

Shane glanced from Poor Boy to the female prisoner and then he shrugged. "It's as good a name as any. I'd just hate to see bounty hunters coming to claim you. The poster does say dead or alive. Some of those hunters can be a bit…how can I say this? They are outside of the law in the way they gather their bounties. But if you already have a poster on you I guess it doesn't matter."

An eerie shade of white replaced her earlier blush, and Poor Boy took a step toward her. He stopped after one step. There was nothing he could do for her. "Why don't you just sit down and tell us who you are?"

CHAPTER TWO

The familiar ring of the bell over the mercantile door jingled when Poor Boy entered. He took a deep breath cherishing the smells of coffee, cinnamon, and peppermint mixed with a hint of pickles.

"Jumping Jehoshaphat! Ain't you a fine sight!" Cookie boomed as he walked toward him. Cookie hadn't changed one bit. The old cowboy still had a thick head of white hair and a hint of mischief in his blue eyes.

"Cookie, it's great to see you." Poor Boy wrapped his arms around the older man. "Looks like life has treated you well."

"That it has. I finally convinced our Edith to marry me."

"Congratulations! When's the big day?"

Cookie frowned. "All she'll say is someday. But, my boy, it's progress."

Poor Boy nodded. "Yes it is. I'm happy for you both. All of Edith's letters always had news of you. I know how much she cares for you."

"Stop talking about me!" Edith called from the back room. "I can hear you!"

"Best hearing in the whole dang town," Cookie whispered.

"Yes I do," she sang out.

Both men laughed.

"In that case, I'll order from here. I need a new mattress for the jail. The ticking on the one in there is stained something awful."

Edith walked out of the back room, her hands on the back of her hair as though making sure it was still proper. Then she automatically smoothed out her skirt. "That I can do. I have a few straw filled ones in the back."

"Straw will have to do. Also we need new bedding."

Edith's brow furrowed. "Now just who is paying for all this?"

"Oh heck, Edith, you know good and well, Cinders will pay the tab." Cookie motioned to Poor Boy to follow him. "Come on, kid, let's get the mattress while Edith finds the bedding."

"Humph! I don't see why a prisoner should get anything new," Edith said to no one in particular before she went about picking out sheets.

Poor Boy grew warm inside. Some things never changed, and that was a good thing. He'd had so much upheaval in his life. A little sameness was appreciated by him. There'd been a time Edith hadn't liked him and thought him a street urchin but she came around eventually and paid for him to go to school back east. She liked to talk hard but she had a kind heart. Though it seemed the kindness was something only he and Cookie could see.

"I can't wait until you meet Ann Marie! I've told her all about you! You have an education and a booming business now. You can have your pick of any of the finer girls in town. I just know you and Ann Marie will hit it off." Edith smiled as though it was a done deal.

Cookie laughed. "She sure is a pretty young gal. Blond hair and blue eyes, and she's very pleasant. She never gives anyone trouble."

Poor Boy gave a noncommittal smile. She sounded a bit boring, but he'd have to meet her to be sure. "What's her brother like?"

Edith took a step forward. "Aaron is as nice as they come. You remember Peg, Keegan and Addy's girl? She's almost eight now. She has declared that she's going to marry him when she turns ten. She's always been bright for her age, but I think she'll have to wait for more years than she counted on."

"I'm supposing Ilene and Tramp have kids too."

Edith sighed. "The good Lord didn't bless them."

"Perhaps they've been blessed in other ways," Poor Boy said, hoping to end the conversation before Edith had a chance to say something she shouldn't. "I'll take one mattress and the bedding. She had a saddlebag with her. I guess I should have looked to see if she had any clothes or not. I might be back."

Edith rang up the purchases. "I'm keeping a tab. If you see Cinders before I do, make sure he pays me. Cookie, help him carry the mattress."

"No need. I got it. I'll see both of you later."

"I'm glad you're back, kid. Shane could really use your help. Cecily is expecting their third child, and she tires easily. Yep, it sure is good to see ya." Cookie slapped him on the back as he held the door open for him.

Poor Boy crossed the dirt street to the sheriff's office. He entered and was surprised to see Corny asleep on the bunk. Corny… He smiled. What a stubborn woman. He couldn't decide if she was brave or just foolish. How'd she end up robbing a bank? She was so young, and already her life was ruined. It was very possible she'd be hanged. Where was

15

Judge Gleason anyway? He was usually in town. Could be he was playing poker in the saloon. Did Noreen still own it? He hated saloons. Having grown up in one, he understood what a raw deal the women got.

"Can I go to the funeral?" Her words startled him.

"He's already been buried, sorry."

"Already?" She stood and clasped the bars. He felt the pain in her voice.

"They don't waste time. Coffins are ready made, and the ditch digger gets paid. So for them, the sooner the better. I'm sorry. I could make a wooden marker if I had a name."

Her eyes narrowed. "You'd like that wouldn't you?"

"You know at this point it doesn't matter what your name is unless there is a wanted poster on you. I'm telling you for your own good, if there isn't one you need to tell us. There will be bounty hunters sniffing around soon enough." He motioned for her to step back while he put the key into the cell door lock. He closed it behind him then removed the old mattress from the cot and replaced it with the new one. He put the sheets and blanket at the foot of the bed. "I really am sorry about your father." He grabbed up the old bedding and opened the door. He locked it behind him and went out the back door with the stained mattress and sheets.

When he moseyed back in, a big man, wearing a black duster stood up against the bars looking at Corny. Poor Boy drew his gun. "Hold it right there." The metallic click as he cocked the gun added weight to his order.

The newcomer slowly turned. "No need for the gun, son. I was lookin' for someone else. What's her name? I bet I can find some type of bounty on her. Husbands and fathers will usually pay to have their little girls back. Not that she's little by any means if you know what I mean."

"Step away from the prisoner," Poor Boy warned, refusing to back down.

The man put his hands up. "I don't want any trouble. I'll just go off to the telegraph office and see what I can find out." He backed away. "I'll be back when I have an answer. What's your name girl?"

She folded her arms in front of him and clamped her lips shut.

"I'll find out. I always do." He turned and left.

She sighed loudly and slid her gaze to Poor Boy. "I guess you were right about the hunters. My name is Molly McDonagh." She waited as though he'd recognize her name.

"I've been living in New York. Should I know the name?"

"My family was known as the Mean McDonagh Gang."

"So, this probably isn't the first time you've been involved in a robbery."

Her eyes widened. "Yes it is. It's all a big mistake. My brothers never killed anyone, but the next thing I knew we were run out of town with a price on our heads. Not mine exactly but on the men in my family. I had four brothers and my father. They are all dead now. Two were hanged without a trial. One was shot out of his saddle over New Mexico way. My youngest brother caught a fever and died, so then it was just me and Pa."

"And your pa took you on a bank robbery with him? I have to say it doesn't sound innocent to me." Poor Boy took a seat behind the desk and tipped the chair onto its back legs while he contemplated her story.

"There's a man waiting for the money. He tracked us down and threatened us if we didn't pull the job." She set about making the bed. Her hands shook as she did it.

"Why not come into the sheriff's office instead of the bank?"

"He had his gun beaded on us the whole time. He had a room at the saloon. One overlooking the town. My pa and I

17

figured we'd do this, get rid of the man and head down to Mexico."

"Get rid?"

She finished the bed and sat down on it. "Escape, yes. Isn't that what you'd have done?"

He shrugged. "'Get rid of' could mean kill him."

She paled. "Like I said, we never killed anyone. I have a man I'd like to kill, but revenge never serves. One of the sons of the richest man in town pointed the finger at my brother Todd, and then later he included my brother Grey in his accusation. We had to leave our ranch. We'd worked so dang hard to build it, and in an instant it was all taken away. The man who accused my brothers, David Baff, is a mean vindictive man. His family wanted our land and by now they probably have it."

Tears filled her eyes and she quickly dashed them away. "I'm not a big crier. I want you to know that. Fate turned on us, but we kept fighting to stay alive and on the right side of the law until now."

"I'll go over to the saloon and ask around. I'm going to lock the doors to the sheriff's office while I'm gone. It'll be safer that way." He grabbed his hat and placed it on his head. "I appreciate you telling me the truth."

He walked out the door without looking back at Molly. It was a darn shame she'd been at the bank with her father. There wasn't much he could do to save her neck. It was a pretty neck too.

He pushed open the swinging doors to the saloon and ambled inside. Looking around, he made a mental note of who was where. If a fight started, he'd need to know which way to go to get out of the line of fire. Noreen gracefully descended the stairs and gave him a look that made his skin crawl. The last five years had aged her. She'd always had an air of innocence about her, but no more.

Whoring usually aged women before their time. Late nights, his mother had told him when he asked. He figured it was the alcohol and being man handled that gave them a look of hopelessness. It wasn't an easy life.

"Poor Boy, is that you?" Noreen asked as she sidled up next to him.

He made a distinct action of moving away from her. "Hi ya, Noreen. Long time no see."

"It sure has been a while. Why just look at you! You're no longer the dirty street rascal you once were. I'm happy for you!" She took his hand and led him to the bar. "Sandy, pour us some of the finest whiskey we have." She nodded to the burly dark-haired bartender.

Poor Boy almost declined but he wanted her comfortable enough to talk to him. He took a hearty swig of the whiskey and smiled. "I don't think I've ever had anything so smooth, thank you."

"I don't suppose you're here for one of my girls, so what's going on?"

"There was an accomplice in the bank robbery."

"Oh, yes, that pretty young thing you have over in the jail. I'd like to help you out but I don't take criminals on to work here." She leaned over to give him a good look down her dress.

He shuddered in disgust but by Noreen's knowing smile it was obvious she thought he liked the view. "It's not the prisoner I'm talking about. It's about a man who took one of the front rooms. He had a gun trained on the bank. Most likely a rifle but I don't know for sure, yet."

"There was a man. He wanted a room, no company. He was tall, blond, handsome as all get out. He had the biggest brown eyes, and a girl could get lost in them."

"Did he have a name?"

"Yes, it was Drew, short for Andrew."

"What about a last name?"

Noreen blinked at him. "I didn't ask, and he didn't offer. You know how it is Out West."

He nodded. "Yes, I do. If you happen to see him again, could you let me know?"

She winked at him. "Of course, sugar. Don't be a stranger, you hear?"

"Thanks, Noreen. It's good to see you again." He drank down the rest of his whiskey and then left. As he stepped out onto the wooden walk, he shivered. A cold wind had kicked up, and the clouds above looked ominous. He'd planned to spend his spare time visiting with his friends; Cinders, Keegan, and Tramp. At least he'd seen Shane, Edith and Cookie. He sighed. His free time would be spent with Molly. It was bad enough when a girl went bad, but to have her own father involve her in a robbery was intolerable. Shucks, maybe it wasn't her fault. Too bad he couldn't do anything about it.

He walked to the jail and found Shane sitting behind his desk, drinking coffee. "Tell me about the bounty hunter," Shane said.

Poor Boy filled him in, glancing at Molly the whole time. The fear on her face pulled at his heart.

"Best thing to do is get her out of here. I already set a plan in motion. We'll sneak her into the back of a wagon and you can head out to Cinders and Tramp's place. It'll be safer there. Jasper, the foreman, just moved back east, and the house is empty."

"My job is here."

"Your job is to protect the prisoner until Judge Gleason gets back. It shouldn't be more than a week."

Poor Boy nodded. "Don't worry I'll keep her safe. We'd better get going, it's starting to get cold out there, and we'll probably get freezing rain."

"I was thinking the same thing. Cecily is packing some clothes for Molly, and Cookie is getting the wagon ready. Cecily is a bit disappointed. She wanted you to come for dinner, but she understands."

Poor Boy nodded. "There will be plenty of dinners. Give her my best."

"You can do it in person," Cecily said as she came through the door. She put the valise she carried down on Shane's desk and embraced Poor Boy. "What a wonderful man you've become." Tears filled her eyes, and she pulled away and gazed at him. "I've missed you."

"I've missed you too. I hear congratulations are in order for you and Shane." He wasn't sure why so many people were so happy to see him. It was nice and all but a bit overwhelming.

"Yes, thank you. We're very excited. I can't wait for you to meet the others. Molly, it's nice to meet you. I'm Shane's wife. I wish we had time to get to know each other, but I have to get the bag to the mercantile so Cookie can put it in the wagon. You're in good hands." She took the valise and gave Shane a sweet smile. "I'll see you for supper."

If he wasn't mistaken, Poor Boy thought he saw a slight blush creep up Shane's face. It was good to see evidence that love was a lasting thing.

"So what's the cover story? We don't want bounty hunters at the ranch."

Shane stroked his chin. "I was thinking she could be your sister. This way you can share the house and no one will raise an eyebrow. It would be on a need to know basis. Molly Hastings sounds like a good name."

"Except everyone knows I'm an orphan who grew up in a whore house before coming to Asherville."

"Who's to say your mother didn't have another child she

21

put in an orphanage? You somehow discovered you had a sister and you found her. Most people don't ask for details."

"Except for Edith."

"Cookie has sworn her to silence."

"That's going to keep her quiet?" Poor Boy was at a loss. Edith was the biggest gossip in town.

"You'd be surprised at the change in her," Shane said. "She still likes to talk, but she respects what Cookie wants. It's been an entertaining transformation, but I trust her now."

Poor Boy nodded. If Shane trusted Edith, he would too.

There was a knock at the back door. Shane got up in a flurry of movement and rushed to the back and opened it, allowing Cookie to slip in.

"Wagon is ready out back. I got supplies and put canvas over them. We can sneak the gal out of town under the canvas. I got extra blankets too—a storm is brewin'. Let's get cracking." Cookie grabbed Poor Boy's bag and headed out back.

Shane let Molly out of the cell and handed her a cloak and scarf that Cecily had brought for her.

"Here, Poor Boy, take this rifle with you." Shane handed him the rifle and ammunition. "Stay safe. Some of those bounty hunters can be unscrupulous. You take care. You too, Molly. Keep your head low."

Poor Boy gave them both an appreciative nod, and then he led Molly out the back door. Cookie held up the tarp, and Molly quickly got in the wagon and lay down. Cookie placed all but two of the blankets over her and then covered her with the tarp. He handed Poor Boy one of the blankets and wrapped the other one around himself. "Don't you worry, Shane, I'll get them to Cinders and Tramp's place in one piece. Don't forget we're having a Christmas Feast at the ranch."

"You'd best hurry off," Shane advised.

Cookie insisted on driving, and soon they were on their way out of town.

Poor Boy couldn't shake the feeling that they were being watched.

———

MOLLY PRAYED the whole time she was in the back of the jostling wagon. The rain pelted down on the tarp, and Poor Boy had been right, it was freezing rain. How did they fare out there? They must be so cold. On and on they went as it grew colder and colder. Once again, she was the cause of someone else's suffering. It was the dang McDonagh curse. It wasn't only she who caused others' suffering, it was her entire family. Their hardships were put upon others. Without money for food and supplies, stealing had become a way of life. They had all played it off as doing no harm, but she knew they took food off the tables of those who could least afford it at times.

Once she had refused to eat stolen food, but she was so hungry and the deed had already been done. When they'd had their ranch, they'd often fed those down on their luck, but what they'd done wasn't the same. It hadn't been given; it had been stolen. Good deeds were something that came back to a person, not something anyone could just take when needed.

She shivered as she turned onto her other side. Now she was the only McDonagh left. Good and caught, too, with no hope of getting away. They said the judge would be back in a week. She'd have a week to repent and maybe she'd be able to do some small turn of goodness for someone before she was to hang.

23

Christmas had always been such fun while her mother was alive. The boys would cut down a tree and they'd pop corn and string it to put around the tree. Yes, her mother had been a happy soul. She'd sung a lot and she'd had the sweetest smile. Molly sighed. Would she live to see this Christmas? Probably not.

CHAPTER THREE

*C*ookie drew the wagon right up to the foreman's house and both Poor Boy and Cookie jumped down. They lifted the tarp and both sighed in relief when they saw that Molly hadn't frozen to death.

Poor Boy drew the girl into his arms and carried her to the house. Cookie had already rushed inside and was laying wood for a fire. Poor Boy gently put Molly on the couch and soon the cabin was filled with firelight.

"Are you alright?" he asked as he knelt beside her. Her whole body shivered, and it worried him.

"Get her something warm to drink. I'll bring in your things and get these horses settled in the barn. I'll let Cinders and Tramp know what's going on. Don't worry about food. We'll bring some over, and I bet Shannon and Ilene will want to hover over the little gal." Cookie walked back outside and returned with their belongings. "Stay warm."

Poor Boy nodded his thanks. He put the pot filled with water over the fire to boil, and he also put on a pot of coffee. "I'll get you warmed in no time."

"Get yourself warmed up first. You were outside in this

25

weather. I had the blankets and canvas over me." She sat up and rubbed her hands together. "Be sure you don't have frostbite."

"I'm fine but thanks for caring."

Her brow furrowed. "Why wouldn't I care?"

"In my experience, the world isn't made up of caring folks. They care about themselves or their families but not others. The only people I've found to be truly caring are the people here in Asherville." He shook his head. He shouldn't be telling others his problems. "I'm thinking we should have a good story of how we're brother and sister to tell people. Cinders and his wife Shannon as well as Tramp and his wife Ilene are trusted friends, but everyone else will have to be told we're kin."

"Why didn't you just leave me in the jail? The judge is bound to hang me. Why go to all the trouble?" Her blue eyes were so big he found himself getting lost in them.

He walked to the window near the door and peered outside at the ranch he loved. The storm raged on, but all he saw was a place to put down some roots. This was what he wanted, a ranch where people considered themselves to be family. "No trouble, just doing my job. If people thought you were still in town, it would just put Shane in danger with bounty hunters trailing his every move. I'll have to take a look at those wanted posters. It never occurred to me there'd be ones with women on them."

"I never gave it much thought either. It took too much energy to survive for me to be worrying about being wanted. I really thought with my brothers all dead, my pa and me could start a life somewhere, but it wasn't meant to be." Her voice was soft and wistful.

"Coffee should be done by now. Would you like a cup?" He didn't wait for an answer. Instead, he walked across the cabin and took two cups off a makeshift shelf and carried them back to the fire, where he squatted and poured them both a cup.

"Thank you," Molly said as he handed her a cup.

"Are you warm enough? Where did you say you hailed from? These Texas storms can be fierce."

"Pennsylvania originally, and then after the incident we've been all over. I can't rightly say I'm from anywhere anymore. We used to have a lot of snow when I was growing up." She shrugged and took a sip from her cup.

"We don't get as much snow, but the icy rain sure is hard to deal with. I know being here with me isn't the ideal situation. We're just trying to keep you safe is all."

"Oh, it's a lovely cabin."

Glancing around, he smiled. "I've been in plenty worse."

Molly nodded and stared at the fire. What was she thinking? Probably about her father. He sure understood her sadness. He had been heartbroken when the Eats died. Eats had been more of a father to him than anyone. He could only imagine how it felt to have a real father die. Not knowing what to say the silence ensued. He pulled a chair near the fire and sat down until he too stared into the flickering flames.

HER HEART SQUEEZED. Her pa must be so cold in the ground. How was she going to live without him? Worrying about her future helped to crowd out the vision of her dead father. She frowned. There was no sense in worrying about a future she'd never have. Once the judge heard her name and her family's crimes, it would be all over.

She glanced over at the deputy. He made her feel safe. It had been a long time since she'd felt that way. He was so very handsome, and it was just as well she'd be gone. He was probably quick with his gun, and she never wanted a man who could pull a gun on another man in her life again.

There was a knock on the door and she stood her gaze darting around the room seeking somewhere to hide.

"It's fine. Everything is fine," Poor Boy said in a soothing voice.

He went to the door and opened it wide, allowing two women followed by two men to come inside. She stayed as still as possible as they all hugged Poor Boy. He certainly was a popular man. Her heart was happy for him but doubly sad for herself.

"Molly, this is Shannon and Cinders and this is Tramp and Ilene. They own the ranch."

She tried to smile but failed. "It's nice to meet you. Thank you for giving me a place to stay until they hang me." She quickly put her hand over her mouth. "I didn't mean to say the last part."

"Welcome," Cinders said. He was tall with broad shoulders. His blond hair hung past his shoulders.

"I'm so glad you made it here before you all froze," Shannon said. She had a pretty smile. She quickly took off her cloak and bonnet, revealing her brown hair and a prominent scar on the side of her face.

Tramp set a basket on the table. "Cookie sent food." He was a handsome man with brown hair.

"I'm Ilene. It's so nice to meet you." The pretty woman with beautiful blue eyes and curling brown hair sat down next to her. "Are you thawed out from your trip out here?"

"Yes, ma'am. I'm warm now."

"Poor Boy, I can't get over how much you've grown and filled out," Shannon exclaimed causing his face to turn a bright shade of red.

"I'm proud of you," Cinders said. "Now you're the deputy. But don't feel obligated to keep the job. I know you have the restaurant too. Take your time and decide what's best for you."

"So, how real is the danger to Molly?" Tramp asked.

Poor Boy stood tall. "Shane thought it bad enough he sent us out here."

Cinders stared at Molly. "Just how many posters do you have out on you?"

She blinked and then frowned. "None that I know of. My brothers had a few before they were killed. But there seems to be a few posters for female bank robbers and the bounty hunters are coming in to see if I'm one of them. The sheriff was of the mind that some wouldn't much care if I matched the poster exactly or not."

Cinders nodded. "He's right about that. Dead or alive and most would rather not deal with a live prisoner. So, the cover is that you two are brother and sister. We can go along with that easy enough. I've alerted all our men to keep an eye out for strangers. They don't need to know more than that."

"Thank you," she said as she shuddered. It hadn't occurred to her someone would just shoot her and ask questions later.

Tramp shook his head and smiled as he gazed at Poor Boy. "I know everyone has already said it but I can't get over how mature you are now. You left as a skinny kid and look at you now. I don't mean to embarrass you or nothin', but you have to admit it's a big change."

Ilene stood. "I think what he's trying to say is that we all feel as though you're part of our families."

Tramp smiled at Ilene and nodded.

"I think Ilene explained it beautifully," Shannon said. "Make sure you eat and get some rest. I'm sure Cookie will be by in the morning with breakfast. Then if the weather is any better you're welcome to have meals at the house with the rest of us."

"Looking forward to it," Poor Boy said. He helped Ilene with her cloak. "Have a good night."

Molly watched as they all bade them a good night. When the door finally closed, she relaxed her tense body. "They seem like very nice people."

"They are." The affection he held for his friends came through in his voice. "Let's eat."

She went to the table and helped him to unload the basket. It was amazing, the amount of food that had been inside. Fried chicken, fresh bread, boiled potatoes, and even a plate of cookies. "There's enough food here for ten people."

"Cookie is a generous man. Maybe tomorrow we can go to the main house and catch up. They have kids I've never met. It seems strange."

"It's nice they consider you to be family. You must have been quite the little boy."

"I was thin, and my clothes hung on me. I had a hard time sleeping so I looked like a waif, I suppose. They always treated me with respect. I knew how much they meant to me but I never imagined they felt the same way."

"You're a nice man, Poor Boy."

He grinned as they both sat down to eat. "When I was in school in New York they changed my name to Edwin. I hated it. Ed would have been bearable, but Edwin set my teeth to grinding. Poor Boy might be a strange name but it's mine."

"I can understand that. I suggested my family change its last name but they refused. It wasn't them who put the original black mark next to the McDonagh name." She took a bite of the chicken and almost moaned out loud. It was so good, better than her mother's.

"Good, isn't it?"

"You read my mind." They ate the rest of the meal in silence, and after supper, she washed the few dishes and put them back into the basket. Then she went and unpacked the clothes Cecily had gathered for her. Tears came to her eyes at the nightgown and two dresses she found inside. It had been a while since she'd worn a dress. It had been easier to ride with pants on.

Poor Boy poured some of the heated water into a basin and set it along with a bar of soap on the table. "It's been a long day. I'm sure you'll want to wash up. The weather is too bad to get enough water for a bath—"

"This is fine." She smiled at him as she reached out and touched his arm. "You've been so kind to me."

He shifted his weight from one foot to another. "It's easy being kind to you." He took the bucket and walked back to the fire. I'll keep my back turned so you can get dressed for bed."

She'd always imagined there'd be a time when a man would want to see her undressed. Marriage and children had always been in the picture when she thought of what her future would be like. A small sob escaped her. Her future was very different now.

———

POOR BOY ADDED MORE wood to the fire. Sleep wasn't coming any too easy for him. The small couch didn't hold half of his length, and the floor was proving to be a challenge. Molly had insisted he take the bed, but he'd refused. She was sleeping, but it wasn't a restful sleep. She tossed and turned something awful. He watched the shadows the flames tossed against the walls. Poor Molly. Losing her father and facing the hangman must be terrifying. Somehow, she had managed to give him a few smiles. He liked her smiles…maybe a little too much. He needed to keep his distance. After all she was his prisoner.

The sound of frozen rain pelting the outside of the cabin

31

grew louder. It was going to be a big mess tending the animals tomorrow. He'd pitch in to help. Morning came early on a ranch. He lay his head down and closed his eyes.

A scream had him quickly on his feet. It had come from Molly.

He raced to the bed and found her thrashing around, groaning and crying in her sleep. He sat on the bed and gently touched her shoulder, and the stark fear in her eyes when she woke made his heart hurt for her. He reached for her and took her into his arms. Cupping her head in his hand, he guided it to his shoulder.

She shuddered, and her body wracked with sobs. Finally, she put her arms around his neck as though she was holding on for dear life. Her suffering went on for a long while.

He stroked her back as his shirt became soaked with her tears. He held her to him, trying to make her feel safe. Perhaps there was no real way to make her feel that way, but he was going to try. Her sobs began to slow, and he caressed the back of her graceful neck, murmuring to her that everything was going to be all right. He'd only held a woman once, but it was tawdry compared to the rightness of Molly in his arms.

Everything about her was soft and womanly. It had been hard to judge just how womanly she was in the clothes she'd been wearing. A need built up inside him, and he wanted to kiss her, but he didn't have the right. It wouldn't be fair to either one of them. Besides, he was pretty sure she was innocent in the ways of men. But that didn't stop him from breathing in her delightful scent.

She pulled back and gazed at him with her red, puffy eyes. His stomach clenched as he stared at her red lips. They looked so very ripe and ready for the taking. He'd be a fool to kiss her, but everything within him wanted to take the chance. He leaned forward, just a taste... But at the last minute, he stood up and tucked her back in. She wasn't in the right frame of mind to know what she wanted, and he wasn't about to take advantage of her.

"Get some sleep," he said, his voice sounding unnaturally husky. It took a lot, but he walked back to the fire and got down on the floor. He waited for his heart to stop pounding before he lay down and slept.

THE NEXT MORNING was as cold and iced over as he predicted. The window was iced over, and he couldn't see what was going on. He hurried and got dressed. Quickly, he pulled on his boots, jacket, hat, and gloves before he opened the door. One step past the threshold, he went flying on the ice, landing on his rear end at the bottom on the steps with a grunt. Gingerly, he stood back up and carefully punched through the crusted ground with each step to keep from sliding. He laughed when he saw Dill, one of the ranch hands fall on his back. It was going to be one of those days.

"Are you going to go check on the cattle?" Poor Boy asked.

"No, we have men at all of the line shacks. They're within walking distance of the cattle. There's no safe way to ride a horse on this ice."

Poor Boy nodded. There was a whole lot he didn't know about ranching. It never hurt to learn. "Are you going to the main house?"

"Sure am."

"Could you tell Cookie we still have plenty of food from last night and not to risk a bad fall coming over?"

"We?" Dill tilted his head waiting for an answer.

"My sister and I."

Dill looked confused. "You have a sister? Since when?"

Poor Boy chuckled. "I guess since the day she was born. I

had taken off before that. Didn't know about her until recently. Mind telling the guys? Her name is Molly. I don't want her to feel awkward when we come for lunch."

Dill smiled and nodded. "Sure thing. It's nice to have you back." Dill punched through the ice with the heel of his boot as he walked to the main house.

Poor Boy sighed in relief. He wouldn't have to explain Molly to the rest of them and Shannon, Cinders and Cookie could fill in any information the men asked for. Maybe he should keep Molly in the cabin. Once the men saw her, he had a feeling they'd want to get to know her and trouble would end up brewing.

———

MOLLY WOKE FEELING GROGGY. Nightmares plagued her all night. Anxiously she looked around and was relieved she didn't see Poor Boy. It was a chance to get dressed in privacy. Quickly she donned a blue calico dress Cecily had given her. The fit was just right and she smiled in delight. Once dressed she put the coffee on to boil. She walked to the window and was astounded that she couldn't see anything. The ice must have been very thick. Wanting a better look, she opened the front door and gasped. Ice clung to everything. The trees, the ground, the steps, and the sides of the cabin were all covered with glittering hard ice. It didn't appear safe out there, and she blew out a breath she hadn't been aware she was holding when she spotted Poor Boy heading her way.

She watched him walk, digging his heel into the glossy, hard ground first before taking a step. She shook her head in admiration. He always seemed to know the right way to do things. Other than the sound of the ground crunching with each step he took, it was eerily quiet. Where did all the birds go? After scanning the area, she decided they must have fled. Hopefully, they had found a safe place.

She stood in the doorway waiting for Poor Boy and her heart flipped at the big grin he gave her. She'd best be careful or that smile would sweep her off her feet. What was it like to be in love? She smiled back and then her smile slowly faded. She'd never know. Her heart squeezed painfully. All her family was gone and she was alone in the world. It was such a lost lonely feeling. Actually, it was terrifying.

Poor Boy came in and quickly closed the door. "It's cold yet it has a certain beauty about it. I'm supposing Judge Gleason won't make it to town any time soon." He removed his coat, hat, and gloves and then tilted his head studying her. "Are you alright? You tossed and turned all night."

"I'm sorry I woke you. Thank you for giving me comfort. I'm just mourning my father, actually my whole family. One accusation from an unstable man, and my family died for it. I hope the cattle all died out and the grass turns to ash. We worked so hard to build our ranch, and in a split second it was gone." She shrugged and glanced away. "Greed is ruining our world."

He grabbed her hand and pulled her to the couch where they both sat. "Not everyone is greedy. I've seen a lot of both sides of it. There are more good people in the world than there are greedy people. Those people need to realize their actions affect others and not in a good way. There are too many jobless, starving families out there. I wish there was something I could do to help them."

"Keeping the people of Asherville safe is a start."

His face softened at her words, and he nodded. "I propose we have a big breakfast of fried chicken with all the fixin's. We'll go to Cinders' this afternoon. You'll like it there. Their little girl must be about five now. Do you like kids?"

Her semblance of a smile faded. "I love them. I'd always

planned to have many..." She stood and got busy setting out the food. Pity wasn't something she invited and it wasn't something she wanted. "Let's eat."

The heat of his gaze could be felt throughout the whole meal, and she could only imagine how red her face had become. She successfully avoided his gaze the whole time. He was really the type of man she'd hoped to settle down with, well minus the gun on his hip.

"I hope this weather lets up soon. I want to check out Eats' Place. I can't believe I own it. Eats could be a gruff man, but he treated me like his own. It was the occasional out-of-town customers who'd cuff me one. When Eats' first restaurant burned down, Shane and Cecily let me live with them. They treated me like kin. Now, New York City was very different. I went to a school for the more privileged kids. They didn't like one thing about me. Edith gave me the best clothes she knew of, and they weren't good enough. I never let on to her though."

He took a deep breath and fiddled with his fork. "The first three years, I had bruises all over me. There wasn't a day where'd I was left alone except for holidays. Most of the boys went home, but I always stayed. I didn't want Edith to spend any more money on getting me home. I liked the quiet times the best. Then in my fourth year, I grew tall and my shoulders filled out. I was bigger than the kids who had bullied me. I defended myself a few times, and that was that. They left me alone after that."

He stood and walked to the window. "I've never told anyone about it. It was a chance of a lifetime to get some learning. I studied hard and got good grades. Top of my class I was. Edith wanted me to go to college, but I wanted to come home. This is where I want to be."

"I'm glad you told me, and I'm happy for you. The people here really care about you."

He turned and looked at her. "They'll come to like you too."

Her heart dropped as a lump formed in her throat. Why was he acting as though she'd be around for a while? Maybe it was easier than to think about her impending fate. She busied herself cleaning up after their meal. After that, she explored the cabin. There were books on the shelf and a half-finished needlepoint picture.

Picking up a book, she carried it to the fire and sat. Then she opened the book and read for a bit while Poor Boy whittled.

Before long, he jumped up. "I can't stand all this sitting around. I'm going out to the barn. Want to come with me?" He gave her another heart-stopping smile.

"Yes, I would love to." She carefully marked her spot in the book and stood up. Grabbing her boots, hooded cloak and gloves she then put them on. Fresh air sounded inviting.

"Don't forget we're brother and sister. There's bound to be a few ranch hands around."

She nodded. "I'll remember." She followed him out the door and held fast to the hand he offered her. He gave her comfort without seeming to know it.

They slowly and carefully made their way across the ice. She stepped in his footprints and it was much easier. Poor Boy let go of her hand and then opened the door. She took a step forward, and her feet shot out from under her, sending her forward. The next thing she knew she was safe in the strong embrace of her handsome deputy. They stared at each other, and the expression in Poor Boy's gaze surprised her. It was as though he looked at her with love in his eyes but she knew it to be false. Laughing to break the tension, she pulled out of his arms and pretended to be interested in the horses. As long as she lived, she'd never forget the flare in his eyes when he gazed at her.

"Hey, Dill!" Poor Boy greeted.

"This is my sister, Molly. Molly, this is Dill."

Dill smiled deeply. "Howdy, Ma'am. It's nice to meet you." The handsome cowboy said. "Are you married?"

Poor Boy's frown made her smile.

"No, she isn't married. She's not interested in courting or the like. You can pass that tidbit on to the other Romeos around here."

Dill laughed. "It figures. The good ones are always off limits. Speaking of good women, what are your intentions as far as Ann Marie? She's a beaut."

"I haven't met her yet."

Dill whistled through his teeth. "I thought you and her were getting hitched."

Poor Boy shook his head. "Like I said, I haven't set eyes on her. I just found out about her the other day."

"So you wouldn't mind if I asked her to go walking?"

Molly covered her mouth to keep from laughing at Dill's hopeful face. "Let him meet her at least. Does she think she's marrying Poor Boy?"

Dill shrugged.

"That's what I heard," Rollo commented as he strolled into the barn. "I think the happily ever after is already planned, Poor Boy. You know how women can be." He turned to her. "I beg your pardon. But if they want you hog tied, then that's what you're going to be—hog tied." He turned toward Molly. "I'm Rollo."

Poor Boy stepped forward. "This is my sister, Molly, and no she does not want to take a stroll in the moonlight with you."

Rollo chuckled. "Well that's a darn shame. Nice to meet you, Molly. You sure you're related to this cowpoke?"

She froze. Rollo recognized her from town. He had been there when Poor Boy brought her in.

"I'm just askin' because obviously you got all the looks in the family. Besides, Cinders told me the whole story. I saw you in town the day you arrived."

Somehow, she managed to smile, but her body stayed tense. This was going to be much harder than she thought. She'd need some witty replies to have ready for next time. She used to joke with her brothers, but she hadn't had to watch what she said. Lies only led to disaster.

"Molly and I were just about to go to the main house. I want to introduce her to the kids before all you yahoos head in for lunch."

"Nice to meet you, Molly," Rollo said.

"It certainly is," Dill added.

"Nice to meet you both too." She held her hand out to Poor Boy. She'd need his strength to get her through the next few days.

"Whew, I'd forgotten Rollo saw you the day I arrested you. Thank goodness Cinders was able to talk to him before he saw you again."

"You can say that again."

CHAPTER FOUR

$\mathcal{C}$inders and Shannon's house was warm and cozy and full of laughter. Poor Boy sat on a settee with Molly and felt blessed. They watched as the two children played. Olivia was the oldest at five years of age. Her winsome smile was the same one Shannon had, and her blue eyes seemed to take everything in. Her hair was blond like her father's. Then there was Robert, the two-year-old. He toddled after his sister, often falling down into a sitting position. He reminded Poor Boy of Cinders and would probably take right after his dad.

Molly stood and gathered some wooden blocks that were scattered on the wood floor. She took them and sat down in a corner, out of the way of others, and waited until the two children came to her. Her face lit up in delight when Robert plopped down in her lap. There were screeches of delight as they built up the blocks and then knocked them down.

Poor Boy watched as Olivia ran, got her doll, and showed it to Molly. His heart filled as Molly oohed and aahed over the doll, bringing a bright smile to Olivia's face. Looking around, he wasn't the only one who noticed. The house was filled with approval.

He'd only known Molly for such a brief time, but she was somehow becoming important to him. Sighing, he glanced up and found Shannon observing him with a sad smile on her face. She knew what Molly's future most likely would be. His heart squeezed.

Cookie was busy making lunch, but he acted as nervous as a pregnant mare. His mouth formed a grim, straight line. It wasn't like him at all.

"I'm sure Edith is just fine, Cookie," Poor Boy said.

Cookie's eyes widened as he stared at Poor Boy before he nodded. "You're right of course. I'm just fretting like an old woman."

"Is that what old women do, Cookie? They fret?" Shannon chuckled.

"So I've been told."

The door opened, but before Tramp could even get a foot in the door, Cookie sent him back out for more wood. Ilene's eyes filled with humor as Tramp mumbled something before turning back around.

"It's a cold one out there. How'd everyone fair last night? Poor Boy, were you and Molly warm enough?" Ilene took off her wrap, hung it on a peg near the door, and walked over to Cookie as she rolled up her sleeves.

"We were fine, thank you."

Cinders smiled. "Cookie, I think all women fret."

Shannon hit him playfully on the shoulder. "Just for that remark you can help me set the table. The men will be here soon enough."

The other men. Poor Boy would have to spin more lies about Molly. His gut clenched. Lying wasn't something to take lightly and at the same time, he'd never do anything to endanger her.

Molly helped Shannon get the children seated before she took a seat next to him. Tramp came in followed by six other men. The men took off their hats and coats and nodded to Molly before they sat at the table.

Poor Boy waited for the questions but there weren't any. Tramp introduced everyone to Molly and they each nodded and said "Ma'am". Someone must have told them she was his sister and to not ask questions. It worked in his favor. He finally relaxed enough to enjoy the food and the company.

"How long will the ice last?" Molly asked.

Cookie cleared his throat. "You're not from Texas, so you wouldn't know. I've lived here all my life, and I don't know either. You see, God likes to keep us amused by making us guess. It could all be melted by morning or another round of ice could cover us. Hard to tell. I'm lucky enough I can feel the bad weather coming. These old bones of mine are fine at telling me when a storm is coming. That's why being a man is best. We can tell things like this."

Poor Boy saw a lot of twitching of lips as he peered around table. Cookie was always entertaining, but he was one of the best men he knew. He was a man you could count on, and he seemed to know more than most what was right from wrong.

The cowboys all got up, thanked Cookie, and left. Rollo turned and winked at Molly, and then he quickly left. Rollo was beginning to leave a bad taste in Poor Boy's mouth. He glanced at Molly and saw that she'd turned a beautiful shade of red. He mentally shook himself. She was his prisoner, nothing else.

He drank his coffee, listening to Tramp and Cinders making plans for the next few days in case the weather grew worse. Finally, Cookie sat down and joined them. "The ice will be gone by late evening."

It amazed Poor Boy that they all took Cookie's word for it. "How do you know?" he asked.

"My leg is feeling much better. The aches are going away."

A smile tugged at Poor Boy's lips. Real life was obviously more educational than school ever had been. "Good to know."

"Tomorrow I'm supposed to bring you to town to see the restaurant," Cookie told him.

"No can do. I have Molly to look after. I have my orders from Shane."

"I have *my* orders from Edith. We'll figure something out. Edith trumps Shane every time." Cookie shrugged.

"You can't really believe that." Poor boy turned the corner of his mouth down.

"It's easier, if you ask me. But I do see your point. I'll bring Ann Marie to you."

"Whoa. I don't know what everyone has planned for me, but I'm my own man. I make my own decisions, and that includes women. I don't need one or want one in my life right now. I also take offense to the fact that the men think we're getting married. I have never met this Ann Marie. I know nothing about her." He felt Molly stiffen at his side.

"You'll get to meet her tomorrow, and then you can take the rest from there." Cookie stood and piled all the plates for washing.

Poor Boy sighed. "It looked like tomorrow he was meeting Ann Marie.

THE SOUND of the ice melting started that afternoon and water dripped from the roof long into the night. Molly laughed with Poor Boy about Cookie's weather predicting leg. She could tell he had a lot on his mind. He was preoccupied and didn't immediately answer her. Finally, she gave up having any type of conversation with him. Perhaps he was anticipating meeting Ann Marie.

A lump formed in her throat. Telling herself she was happy for Poor Boy didn't help at all. He deserved happiness, he really did. If these were her last days on earth, she was glad she was spending them with him. She could be spending them in the jail cell. Tomorrow she'd spend as much time outdoors as she could. She wanted to experience the sun, the wind, and the smells while she still could. She wanted to see the horses and cattle. She wanted to watch the trees sway back and forth.

She didn't want to watch Poor Boy meeting Ann Marie. She was probably beautiful and poised with an education. And the other woman's clothes were bound to be better than hers.

"I'm going to bed. Good night," she said as she walked to the back of the cabin where the bed was. She didn't even check to make sure his back was turned. He was a man of integrity, kindness, and strength, and she was going to miss him.

Finally, she lay in bed and prayed for her soul to go to heaven when she died.

The next morning she woke to an empty cabin. She pulled the blanket around her and padded to the fireplace. A roaring fire was going, and a pot of coffee was sitting among the hot embers. Next, she walked to the front window and was relieved to see that it was early morning. The world appeared wet, but at least it wasn't frozen. She went back to the fire poured herself a cup of coffee and set it on the table to cool while she washed and dressed.

She decided to wear the burgundy dress that Cecily had given her. She didn't want to look like Poor Boy's penniless kin. Quickly, she undressed and put a cloth in the basin of water near her bed. She washed herself and was just about to get dressed when the door swung open.

Foolishly, she turned to see who it was without covering herself. "Oh! Turn around! I don't want you to see me like this!" She grabbed her blanket and wrapped herself in it. "You didn't see anything, did you?"

Poor Boy just walked back out the door, closing the door firmly behind him.

Oh dear, he'd seen everything, and she had shamed not only herself but him too. Her shoulders slumped, and an overwhelming desire to cry came over her. She quickly grabbed her clothes and got dressed. There wasn't time for tears. They were expected at Cinders' for breakfast, and then Ann Marie would most likely make her debut.

As soon as she was ready, she opened the door and smiled when she saw Poor Boy whittling on the front steps. He glanced at her over his shoulder.

"All dressed?"

She nodded and stepped back so he could come inside. "I'm sorry, I didn't think to lock the door," she said in a quiet voice.

"It's my fault. I should have knocked but in my defense, I thought you were sleeping. No harm done."

She wished she could believe him, but a telltale blush crept up his cheeks. Not knowing what to say, she stared at her feet. The silence was awkward, and it was a big relief when Poor Boy suggested they head over to the main house.

It turned out to be a more jovial meal, with everyone talking and sharing stories. The lovesick gleam in Rollo's eyes worried her, and she moved her chair so close to Poor Boy's, their knees touched. Poor Boy scowled at her, but she didn't care. She knew nothing about this cowboy, and her father usually made sure no one stared at her. Rollo seemed nice enough, but she wasn't interested, and his boldness disturbed her.

As soon as the meal was done, she offered to help with the dishes, but her offer was politely refused by Cookie. She turned and walked out the door instead, with Poor Boy right behind her.

"You don't suppose they don't like me do you?"

He linked his arm with hers. "How could anyone help but like you?

She stumbled, and Poor Boy caught her. He held her to him until she regained her balance. Looking up, she gazed into his eyes. He cared for her. It was right there for her to see. But that only made her sadder. Thoughts of what could have been made her heart heavy. She took a step back and turned toward a wooded area a little ways away from the houses.

"Do you think we could take a walk in the woods? I might not see the outside world after Judge Gleason gets here. I want to feel the earth alive all around me."

"Of course. It's muddy, but what's a little mud? Let's go." He held his hand out to her and she clasped it as if it was a lifeline.

They laughed as the mud tried to suck their shoes in. After going several yards they were completely alone in the woods and she closed her eyes. She listened as birds sang and squirrels ran up and down trees. Even the buzzing of a bee delighted her. The wet mud was pungent, but it was tempered with the crisp scent of the pines. Opening her eyes, she stared up and marveled at the way the sun streamed through the tall trees. She took many deep breaths wanting to remember nature in case she was stuck in a cell for the rest of her life. Or…worse.

"You're shaking," Poor Boy said as he took her into his arms, warming her.

She'd never known anyone like him. He was so kind and gentle, and he sensed her moods and thoughts. She placed her cheek against his chest and heard the thumping of his heart. Life was so very precious and hers might be done soon. Tears filled her eyes at the unfairness of it all. She had finally found someone she could love with her whole being, but it wasn't to be.

He framed her face with his hands and stared into her eyes. "Aw honey, I know you're scared. I wish I could tell you that everything would be fine, but I don't know what will happen." He leaned down and brushed his lips against hers. They both had their eyes open, and the tenderness she saw made her heart squeeze.

He pressed his lips to hers and kissed her soundly. She never thought of a man's lips as being soft before. He tilted his head and coaxed her mouth open. She jumped when he slipped his tongue past her lips, but soon she relaxed and found it to be blissful. His moan of pleasure filled her with happiness, and she wished with all her heart she wouldn't have to leave so soon.

<hr />

POOR BOY WAS STILL WALKING tall after the kiss when he heard a wagon pull up. "I'm here with you, no matter what happens. There is no sense having them come looking for us."

She nodded. "Of course, you're right. Let's go."

He clasped her hand in his as they walked through the woods and back to the main area of the ranch. He saw Edith with a man and women. It must be Aaron and Ann Marie Pike. He frowned. He didn't go for matchmaking even if it was Edith doing the matching. Molly tried to snatch her hand back, but he held on tight.

"We might as well go and meet the Pikes. They have been running my restaurant after all. Heck, we might actually like them. I wouldn't have had any qualms, but with Edith and her plans for me and Ann Marie, it doesn't sit right with me."

"You might actually like her." She pulled him to a stop. "Poor Boy, don't put your life on hold or make any decisions because of me. I'll only be here for a very brief time. Ann Marie will be here long after I'm gone." Her voice became thick, and he hurt for her.

"Let's just go meet them." He started them walking again. "I would like to hear how the restaurant is going. I still can't believe Edith held onto it for me."

"Edith knows who I am. Will she give me away?"

"And taint my good name? She wants me to marry, so she'll be quiet."

They continued to walk until they came to the main house. He gave her hand one last squeeze before letting it go. They walked up the porch steps and opened the door. Edith frowned at Molly before she made a beeline for Poor Boy. She pulled his head down so she could kiss him on the cheek. Heat suffused his whole face.

"Here he is! Isn't he as handsome as I told you, Ann Marie?" Edith beamed while Ann Marie looked decidedly uncomfortable. "Poor Boy, this is Ann Marie and Aaron Pike."

Aaron stuck out his hand and Poor Boy shook it. "Nice to meet you, Aaron and you too, Miss Pike."

"Please call me Ann Marie," she gave him a sweet smile.

"This is my sister, Molly."

"Molly, hello. What a pretty name," Ann Marie said.

"Yes, it's very nice to meet you, Molly," Aaron said with an appreciative look in his eye.

Molly nodded as Poor Boy sized up Aaron. He already

didn't like him. He had a glint in his brown eyes that didn't sit right with Poor Boy.

"Come in," Shannon said graciously. "It's always nice to have visitors. Hello, Aaron. Hello, Molly. It's nice to see you again. Edith, you look lovely today."

Edith narrowed her eyes at Shannon as if wondering why Shannon was being so nice to her. Edith had caused Shannon an awful lot of grief when Shannon had first come to town.

"Thank you," Edith replied stiffly. "Is Cookie around?"

"Of course I am. I skedaddled over as soon as I heard the wagon drive up." Cookie hurried to Edith's side and gave her a quick kiss on the cheek.

The affection between the two surprised Poor Boy. He'd never pictured Edith allowing a show of affection in the company of others. Things sure had changed since he'd been gone.

"Cookie, I was hoping we could have some of that tea I gave you last week," Edith said.

"Of course you can, and I have some cookies to go with it. I was hoping you'd come out today."

"Molly, would you mind helping us?" Edith asked. "Aaron, why don't you sit in this chair, and Ann Marie and Poor Boy you can share the settee."

Edith didn't fool Poor Boy for a second, but he did as she bade. He waited for Ann Marie to sit, and then he took his seat next to her. He had to admit she was lovely. Her hair was honey blond, and her blue eyes looked almost purple. She had a nice smile too. Both she and Aaron shared the same coloring.

"Edith has told us so much about you, Poor Boy. I feel as though I already know you," Ann Marie said. There was kindness in her eyes and he liked that.

"Are you planning to take control of the restaurant?" Aaron asked.

"Aaron, we're not here to talk about Eats' Place. We're here on a social visit," Ann Marie gently scolded her brother.

Poor Boy didn't miss the anger in Aaron's eyes. Didn't the siblings get along?

"Aaron, to tell you the truth I didn't know about Eats' still being open until the other day. It's been a lot to take in, and I haven't given it much thought. As a deputy, I'm not sure how much time I'd have to run the place. We'll have to wait and see."

Aaron frowned. Did he want the restaurant for himself?

Shannon excused herself and went to check on the napping children. Edith sat down in a chair next to Poor Boy, leaving an empty seat next to Aaron. He watched as Molly came in with a plate of cookies. She put them on the table and looked at the empty chair then at Aaron. Her lips formed a straight line and wariness flashed in her eyes. She sat down, and Poor Boy wanted to laugh at how she sat leaning away from Aaron.

"I've got the tea, folks," Cookie said as he set a tray of tin cups and the coffee pot on the table next to the cookies. He pulled a wooden chair over from the table and sat next to Edith. "Aaron and Ann Marie have done a great job with Eats' Place. They added to the menu and you don't have to eat the meal of the day. You have choices and people seem to like it. I've eaten there a few times and they cook almost as good as I do."

"That's quite the compliment, Cookie," Aaron said.

"Yes, indeed." Poor Boy nodded. He leaned forward and accepted the cup of tea Edith had poured for him.

"Ann Marie cooks and waits tables. She helps take care of the books. She's a very accomplished woman," Edith enthused as she stared at Poor Boy.

"How nice," Poor Boy said. *Dang it all!* What was he supposed to say?

"Being the deputy is a dangerous job. You don't have to worry about the restaurant at all. We have it all under control. Don't we, Ann Marie? We have a big crowd every night. With a daring job, you need to focus on that and not worry about Eats." Aaron smiled but it didn't reflect in his eyes. There was something off about that man.

"I can't believe it's almost Christmas," Ann Marie said. "I just love Christmas! Don't you, Poor Boy?"

He didn't like the way they excluded Molly from the conversation. "Molly and I plan to enjoy our first one together. I'm really looking forward to it. I'm thinking of getting a tree for the cabin."

"What fun!" Edith exclaimed. "We'd love to help decorate. Wouldn't we, Ann Marie?"

"Oh yes! We could have a tree decorating party! What do you think, Aaron?"

Aaron raked his gaze over Molly. "I think it would be a fine idea."

Molly shuddered and then took a drink of her tea. She had enough on her mind and didn't need the extra worry of a Christmas party.

"We just moved in and we're still unpacking," Poor Boy said.

"You don't need much," Edith insisted. "How about tomorrow evening? It'll be such fun! Mind you, it's a small place so it'll just be us."

Ann Marie turned toward Poor Boy. "I can't wait."

He put on a smile. "Neither can we. Isn't that right, Molly?"

His gaze locked with Molly's, and his lips twitched. She looked fit to be tied. "I haven't had a tree in a long time." The sadness in her voice stole all his humor. She might not be here when Christmas arrived. He gave her a reassuring smile.

Putting his cup down on the table, he then stood. "Molly

is still weary from all the traveling we did to get back to Texas. I think we should let her rest. It was nice to meet you." His heart swelled at the grateful smile Molly bestowed on him. Holding out his hand, he helped her up and then led her out of the house.

"Aaron seems very nice," Poor Boy teased. "Ouch," he teased some more when she tapped his side with her elbow.

"He's strange, and I don't like the way he looks at me. It's very different from the way Rollo looks at me. Heck, Rollo's stare is very respectful compared to that slime Aaron. He kept staring at my…well my…umm."

"I saw where he was staring. He's no gentleman, though he wants me to think he is."

"Well, they will be here tomorrow for a party. Is it selfish that I did want to put up a tree but with just you and me? Edith and Cookie are coming, aren't they?"

He shrugged. "I have no idea. I can't imagine Edith wanting to miss it."

Molly chuckled. "You're right about that."

They walked into the cabin and stared at each other until Molly broke it off.

"I really am tired," she said.

"I'll let you take a nap then."

"Poor Boy, do you think you could hold me until I fall asleep? I'm just so darn scared. If I go to prison, I want to be able to remember what it felt like to have your arms around me. If I die I want my last thoughts to be of the comfort you gave me."

He swallowed hard. No matter what, he was going to get hurt, but he couldn't deny her request. He wanted to make the same memories for himself. He nodded, and she smiled as he followed her to the bed.

Molly took off her shoes and settled herself on the mattress. He did the same and then, lying on his back, he pulled her into his arms. He kissed her temple and held her, caressing her back and her hair until he heard the sound of her even breathing. His chest tightened. He was going to miss her when she was gone. He'd never known a woman so real before. She made no pretenses, well except for when she'd said she was Corny Cornelius. He smiled. Yes, she was one of a kind.

he next day dawned, and Molly sat on the bed biting her bottom lip, trying to figure out what was involved with a tree trimming party. She was out of her element. Her family had always celebrated together. There were enough of them that they didn't invite guests. Bittersweet memories filled her. They'd been such a happy family. Now she was alone.

She stood up and started straightening the cabin, not that there was a mess but keeping busy sometimes kept her nervousness at bay. Poor Boy slept in front of the fire and the peaceful look on his face was like a tonic to her soul. He'd be with her and everything would be fine. It wasn't as though she'd ever live in this town or get to really know its people.

Tears filled her eyes as her peacefulness disappeared. She turned away and quickly went back toward the bed and got dressed, glancing over her shoulder often to be sure he wasn't awake. Grabbing her wrap, she quietly opened the door, stepped out into the chilled air and sat on the front stairs.

The rising sun was a beautiful sight and she tried to keep

the knowledge that she didn't have many more to view at bay. Life was for the living and for right now, she was still alive and somewhat free. Poor Boy never made her feel like a prisoner and she was grateful. Her life had taken many twists and turns in the last few years but she never thought she'd end up waiting on a judge to decide her fate.

She had been part of the bank robbery, and for some reason, before it happened, she'd never given the fact that other people could have been killed a thought. Now she was left to wonder if any of her brothers had had to kill an innocent person. Hopefully their souls were at peace and they had nothing so heinous to repent for.

Her nose grew cold and it struck her as funny. Usually her hands felt the cold first. The observations she made now were so different from what she usually thought about. She watched as Cookie hustled to the main house and entered without knocking on the door. It was nice they were all part of a big family. They all genuinely enjoyed each other's company.

Christmas was coming, and it wasn't a time to feel sorry for herself. It was a time to celebrate the birth of the son of God. That was what mattered. She'd either celebrate on earth or in heaven. Her fate was no longer in her hands. Smiling, she watched as the sky grew lighter. It would be a good day.

Six hours later, she decided she was so very wrong. All three of them, Edith, Aaron and Ann Marie arrived right after lunch. They all gathered inside the main house, and Edith started the visit off with eye-narrowed stares, which added to Molly's unease. Edith also drew her away from Poor Boy at every turn, allowing him to spend more time with Ann Marie.

Molly's only consolation was that Poor Boy looked as

uncomfortable as she felt. She watched as Ann Marie took every opportunity to brush up against the deputy. Meanwhile, Aaron kept giving her an eerie grin.

"Are you going to cut down a tree? You should do it now before it gets dark," Shannon said.

Poor Boy stood. "Aaron, I'll grab the axe and we can go." Poor Boy's hair practically stood on end from running his fingers through it. A telltale sign he wasn't happy with the way things had been progressing. Molly hid her smile behind her hand.

"What fun!" Ann Marie enthused as she jumped up and grabbed her cloak. She handed it to Poor Boy for him to put it on her.

Molly started to stand.

"Molly, perhaps you could help wash the teacups," Edith suggested, but by the glare she gave, Molly knew it wasn't a suggestion.

Not sure what to do, she sat back down and clasped her hands in front of her. Edith was probably right. She'd just be in the way.

Shannon opened her mouth, but before she could say a word, Poor Boy walked to where Molly sat and reached down, taking her hand in his. "I wouldn't dream of leaving Molly out of the fun. If need be, I'll wash the cups myself when we get back." He pulled Molly up, gave her a quick grin, and led her to where she'd hung her wrap. He took it off the peg and put it gently over her shoulders.

"Have fun!" Shannon called as they went out the door.

Molly took a deep breath. "Do you think we'll get snow for Christmas?" she asked as they walked toward a grove of pine trees.

"Does it feel like it's going to snow?" Ann Marie asked. "It's getting warmer by the hour."

Molly didn't answer her; she just kept plowing ahead.

Ann Marie could be a big pain in the neck. Molly's shoulders were so tight with tension, they'd begun to hurt, but they relaxed as she realized it didn't matter what Ann Marie, Aaron or Edith thought.

"Poor Boy, which tree does you think we should chop?" Molly asked turning in a circle admiring all the trees around them.

"How about that one?" He pointed to one that wasn't too tall.

"That's not a good tree at all," Ann Marie said. "You need to make sure the branches are nice and full." She walked for a bit, examining tree after tree until she found one she liked. "This is the one."

Without waiting for a consensus, Aaron took the axe and began to chop the tree down. He wasn't at it for very long before he became winded and announced he was taking a rest.

Poor Boy took off his coat, put on his work gloves, and grabbed the axe from Aaron. It only took him a couple of powerful swings before the tree came crashing down. The smile on Poor Boy's face was worth putting up with Ann Marie and Aaron for. She'd seen him smile before, but this one was one of joy. His smile was contagious as was his happiness.

"Let's drag it home," Poor Boy said as he grabbed part of the tree.

"I'm still tired," Aaron complained.

"I'll help you," Molly said not waiting for Ann Marie's answer.

The tree was big, and they could have used the siblings' help. How was it they supposedly worked wonders at Poor Boy's restaurant, but here they acted lazy? Something wasn't right with these two. Molly shrugged. They weren't her problem.

They pushed and pulled, and finally they got the tree inside the cabin. Poor Boy made a small wood stand, and the tree was gorgeous with its majestic branches. It took up more room than she thought seemed practical, but it would be fine.

Cookie had left popcorn and cranberries on the table for them to string. Molly sat and began to string the popcorn. Ann Marie plopped herself down on the couch and watched.

"Why don't you help? There's plenty of popped corn." Molly stared at the other woman.

"I don't know how."

"It's easy, really. I can show you," Molly offered.

"I'd rather just watch." Ann Marie turned away from Molly and kept her gaze on Poor Boy.

Poor Boy drew a chair alongside Molly, grabbed the needle and thread, and began stringing the popped corn adding in a cranberry every so often. Molly laughed when it was apparent that Poor Boy was actually eating more than he strung. He gave her a heart-gripping smile while he winked at her.

Ann Marie crossed her arms in front of her as she continued to stare. "Poor Boy, would you like to take a walk with me?"

"Thanks for the offer, but I'm helping Molly. It seems everyone else just wanted to watch." He gazed at Ann Marie and then at Aaron.

"Got anything to drink around here?" Aaron asked.

"I could make us some coffee if you like," Molly offered.

"No, I meant whiskey or the like."

Poor Boy shook his head. "Sorry, we just moved in. We have coffee or water."

Aaron frowned. "I thought this was going to be a party. I'll help string the popped corn so you can take my sister for a walk. I'd like to get to know your sister better."

Ann Marie stood and grabbed her cloak as if it was all settled. Poor Boy did not appear happy as he stood up to follow. "We'll be back shortly."

As soon as they left Aaron sat down next to Molly. "I'm glad they're gone. I don't think your brother approves of me. I don't know what he has stuck in his craw, but he needs to remove it."

Her body tensed at the way he spoke about Poor Boy. "If you want to grab a needle I can help you thread it."

Aaron laughed and pulled a flask out of his pocket. "We might as well have fun while they're away." He took a big swig off his flask and offered it to her.

"What is it?"

"Whiskey, of course. The very best, not at all like that nasty saloon swill. Here have some." He pushed the flask into her hand.

"I don't like whiskey, sorry. Why did you ask if we had whiskey if you had your own?" Aaron shrugged, took the flask back and poured more whiskey down his throat. "Damn good stuff. I wanted to be sure to have mine for the ride home."

"You might as well save the rest. It is a long ride. Would you like to sing Christmas Carols?"

Taking yet another drink, he shook his head. "The first time I saw you, I was enchanted. How about a kiss before your brother comes back?"

Her heart sped up, and she stood. Walking behind the table, she hoped to keep some distance between them. *The nerve of the man.* He stood and stared at her with glassy eyes. He'd imbibed more than he should have. Perhaps she could outrun him and get away.

She tried to move around the table, but he blocked her path. She then tried to move the other way, only to be blocked again. He wasn't going to let her go. She sighed and

60

then tried to smile.

"I think I'd like a drink after all."

Aaron grinned. "I knew you'd change your mind." He reached over the table and handed her his flask. She drank a small amount before she spat it out. How foul tasting. She glanced at him and was uneasy at his narrowed eyes. She turned the flask upside down and poured out the rest of the stinking whiskey.

"You little bitch! That was mine." He lunged over the table, grabbed his flask, and slapped her face. "I'll teach you to ruin things that don't belong to you."

The loud crack of his hand hitting her face echoed in her ears. She put her hand to her cheek and realized her lip was bleeding. It hurt and throbbed. "Get out!"

He slapped her again on the other side of her face. "You don't talk to me that way. Do you understand?"

"Yes, I understand." She hoped and prayed Poor Boy would return quickly.

Aaron stepped in front of her and cupped her cheeks with his hands. Leaning down he kissed her. It was repugnant, and she kneed him in the groin. He went down moaning in pain. Quickly, she ran out the cabin and toward the main house. She didn't knock; she went right in and locked the door behind her. She trembled as she burst out crying.

Shannon hurried to her side. "Who did this to you?"

"Aaron. It was Aaron."

Edith stood and crossed her arms in front of her. "What did you do to make him hit you?"

"Edith—" Shannon started.

"No, she must have provoked him. I've known Aaron for well over a year, and he's good people. He doesn't have a mean bone in his body."

Cinders headed their way and lifted Molly into his brawny arms. He carried her to the couch and laid her down.

"No woman deserves to be hit. What happened, and where is Poor Boy?"

"Poor Boy went for a walk with Ann Marie, leaving me with Aaron. Aaron had a flask of whiskey on him and he drank a lot of it. He wanted to kiss me, and I poured his whiskey out. That made him mad, and he struck me. I told him to get out, and he hit me again. He started to kiss me, and I kneed him. I ran here as fast as I could."

Cinders gave her hand a quick squeeze. "I'll take care of it." He headed to the door. "Be prepared, I might have to hurt him," he told Shannon.

Edith gasped and placed her hand over her heart when Cinders left. "He'd better not put a hand on that boy."

"He's no boy. He's a no-good man," Molly said miserably.

Shannon's eyes narrowed. "Edith, have you looked at Molly's face? No woman deserves to be hit. Maybe you don't know Aaron as well as you think you do."

"Now see here—"

"What in tarnation is going on?" Cookie asked. There'd been so much arguing, no one heard him come in. "What's all the yellin' about?" Before anyone could answer, Cookie's gaze fell on Molly's face. "Oh no." He quickly went and put two cloths into a bucket of water, wrung them out and sat down next to the couch. He placed one cool cloth on one cheek while he dabbed at her bloody lip with the other. "What low-down polecat did this?"

"It was Aaron Pike," Shannon said quietly.

"He didn't take advantage of you, did he?" Cookie asked.

Molly's face heated. "No, I got away before he could."

"You have no indication that he would have attacked you," Edith insisted.

"He tried to kiss me. I got away before he could." Molly's patience had reached its end.

"I'd still like to hear his side of the story," Edith insisted. "Why were you alone in the house with him?"

"I already told you!" She stood up, grabbed her cloak, and flew out the door. No one believed her. She was neither a thief nor a liar, yet she'd been branded as one. It cut to the core. They didn't know her, so her word counted for nothing. She darted to the side of the house and vomited. She could understand being blamed for the robbery, but not for Aaron's attack. She was the victim but that wasn't the way Edith saw it.

Tears ran down her face, stinging places where her skin was broken. Her word meant nothing. She tried to compose herself and then she walked towards the woods again. She needed to be alone. How could Poor Boy have left her with Aaron? He must really be taken by Ann Marie. Damn, she was jealous. Though she wouldn't be around long, she had started to think of him as hers. It was selfish of her. Poor Boy had his whole life ahead of him. He deserved to be happy.

She walked and walked until the sky was no longer visible. In her teary-eyed state, she hadn't paid much attention to the direction she was going. Turning around she walked back the way she had come, but nothing looked familiar. She leaned against a big boulder and shook her head. She hadn't passed a boulder the whole time she had walked. Even with tears in her eyes, she would have noticed. But at least she could see the sky. Not a lot of it but enough to figure out which way was west.

Her father had taught her a lot of useful things. She could make a fire and feed herself if she ever got stranded alone. Hopefully, it wouldn't come to that. If she could keep west she'd be fine, but the sky was hidden in lots of places. She'd need to mark her path. If worse came to worst she'd want the boulders against her back when it got dark.

POOR BOY CURSED under his breath as he raced to the woods. He didn't want to hear any of Aaron's explanations or Edith's accusations. Molly was out in the woods alone. Didn't she think about bears or wolves? She could trip and fall. The moment he heard Aaron's story, Poor Boy knew him for a liar. Molly would never be so forward, it was so wrong to hit a woman.

He wanted to pound Aaron's head against the log cabin, but he needed to rescue Molly first. He hoped they just went back to town. He shuddered. Ann Marie had tried everything to get him to kiss her. She'd even said she had something in her eye and wanted him to check. Did she think he was stupid? Edith had put too many ideas into that girl's head. She told him they were practically engaged.

No one was going to tie him down. He was rope-free and intended to stay that way. As a deputy, he needed to get a place closer to town. Since it would be just him, he wasn't concerned. He'd find something. Cinders had already told him he could have his choice of horse, and he'd seen a couple he was interested in.

He'd been walking for a while now without a sign of Molly. Where'd she get to? Aaron had claimed to have given her no more than a light tap to her cheek, but from the look on Shannon and Cinders' faces, Poor Boy could tell it was more than that. He'd thought Edith had changed her judgmental ways but obviously not. It had hurt when she told him Molly was a no-good thief who should hang from a rope.

Heck, if they hadn't pushed Ann Marie on him, he might have liked to have gotten to know her, but now he wanted nothing to do with either of the Pikes.

Spotting a bent twig, he leaned over and examined it. He

panned the area until he found another like it. He smiled. He'd caught her trail. She was marking it on purpose. Very impressive. But what direction was she going? North, it seemed. He continued to follow the trail, running when the ground was flat. The sun would be setting soon, he needed to find her fast.

He walked almost another hour, she was walking in circles. The temperature started to drop, and he was afraid he wouldn't find her that night. He began to run again, keeping his eyes open for any trail markers. He finally saw a flicker of a fire in the distance. Hopefully, it was Molly and not some dangerous stranger. He approached the fire slowly and silently. A smile pulled his lips upward when he recognized Molly, looking very rumpled sitting in front of a fire cooking what looked to be rabbit. She must carry a knife with her. He'd never noticed before.

"Molly! It's me, Poor Boy. I'm coming into your camp and I'm alone. You have no reason to be afraid." He cautiously stepped into the circle of fire light. "I've had a heck of a time finding you. I'm glad you marked the trail…" He knelt down in front of her. "What the heck happened to your face?" Anger bubbled up inside him. Reaching out, he stroked one of her fiery red cheeks with the back of his hand. He winced when he saw her lip.

"I'm fine, really I am." She looked at him, not in the face but just left of his ear.

"What happened?"

"Aaron wanted something I refused to give, and it made him angry, very angry." Her voice was flat. "He had a flask of whiskey and insisted I drink some. I poured it out instead and he hit me. I told him to leave he slapped me again then he tried to kiss me." She trembled. "I kneed him in, well you know where, and then I ran."

"I shouldn't have left you alone with him. This is my fault."

"No, it's not your fault at all, and it's not mine either. He had no right to try to steal a kiss. None."

"It looks painful." Poor Boy sympathized.

"Which part?" Molly asked.

"All of it."

"You're just in time for supper. I caught a rabbit." She smiled then winced. "It hurts to smile."

"Look at you, a regular pioneer woman. I don't know many women who can catch, skin, and cook a rabbit. You seem very comfortable out here in the woods."

She nodded. "I've had to learn over the years."

He sat on the ground next to her. "We're not far from the cabin. You circled around twice."

"I was afraid of that. We can eat then go back to the cabin if you like."

He nodded. "I'm so sorry for what happened to you. I shouldn't have left you alone. Ann Marie wanted kisses and promises of marriage. Edith put too many ideas in that girl's head."

"Edith let me know that Aaron attacking me was my fault. That's why I ran. I couldn't breathe in there." Her shoulders slumped.

"I used to have nightmares, and I'd run for miles in all kinds of weather. Eventually the nightmares stopped. But I know that exact feeling of needing to get outside to breathe. None of this is your fault. I'd like to wallop Aaron for what he did to you." He stared at her face. "It hurts doesn't it?"

"It stings on one side and throbs on the other, and my lip just plain hurts. But I'll be fine." She took a piece of rabbit off the spit and handed it to him before she took a piece for herself.

It melted in his mouth. "This is exceptionally good. I guess we didn't get a chance to decorate the tree."

"We can easily do it when we get back home." She handed him more rabbit.

Home...he let the word spread over him. There was a pleasant warmth that went with that word. The only place he'd ever considered home was with Eats. It had been a one-room place, but it was warm. During his time in New York, he had known it was temporary, so he'd never tried to make it feel like home. He sat up straighter, shaking off his feelings. The cabin wasn't his home either.

"Was there any word about the judge? Is he back yet?"

He wished he had the words to tell her everything would be fine but he didn't. He didn't have a clue how Judge Gleason would handle the whole thing. "I'm sure Edith would have told us if he had. Thank you for a splendid supper. He stood and held out his hand. She grasped it and he pulled her into a standing position. She ended up standing so very close to him. If her lip wasn't swollen he'd have kissed her. Damn, he was thinking about kissing her too much.

He held her hand the whole way back wishing he had the right words to say but the only words they both wanted to hear was that she wasn't going to hang. He wanted Judge Gleason to make it back quickly but at the same time, he hoped that day would never come. He squeezed her hand and hurried on. He had never been a dreamer, and it wouldn't do for him to start now.

CHAPTER SIX

"I can't go to breakfast looking like this," Molly told Poor Boy the next morning.

"I'm sorry it happened to you, but you have to eat."

She sighed and put down the small mirror she had found on a shelf in the cabin. "You're right. There's no sense hiding out because of that lowdown scoundrel. Just don't leave my side. Promise?"

He gave her a quick nod. "Promise." He put on his coat and then held out her cloak for her. He helped her put it on, and off they went to the main cabin.

They went inside, and Molly's heart dropped. She should have stayed in the small cabin. From the moment she crossed the threshold, all eyes were upon her. There were too many gasps to count, and a great deal of whispering. She tried to turn around and leave but Poor Boy held her fast. She tried to glare at him, but the courage she saw in his eyes was enough to extend to her. She could be brave too.

"Good morning." She made her way to her chair, quickly sat down, and ducked her head. Her courage only went so far. She swallowed hard as Poor Boy sat next to her.

"What the hell—ah, heck happened to you?" Rollo asked in an angry voice.

She raised her head and wished she could hide. "Aaron Pike is what happened to me. I know you all think of him as a gentleman but he's not."

"He hit you?" Rollo jumped to his feet. "Poor Boy, why didn't you arrest him?"

"I didn't know he hit her. I heard he tried to kiss her, but all I knew was she had run out of the house and she needed to be found. I'm as hopping mad as you are. But right now, I need to keep Molly close and safe. I highly doubt Aaron is going anywhere. He's running my restaurant for the moment."

Cookie cocked his brow. "For the moment? Ya want me to go into town and fire him?"

Poor Boy shook his head. "No, but it would have been nice if you'd have put your fist in his face last night."

"Whoa," Cinders said. "Cookie wanted to go after Molly when she ran out last night but we knew you'd find her. The heat of the moment isn't always the best time to act. Like you said, Aaron isn't going anywhere. Judge Gleason should be back today from what I hear. We can file a complaint with him or Shane. It's really whoever we see first."

The blood drained from her face at the mention of Judge Gleason. Her fate would be determined sooner or later. A lump formed in her throat, and she realized her hand was resting against her neck. She was going to hang, and soon.

"Eat up men. I have some salve to put on Molly's face," Shannon said.

"Not Cookie's salve, is it?" Dill asked.

The men looked at each other and cringed.

"Is there something wrong with it?" Molly asked.

"It smells something awful," Rollo said as he shivered.

"It works," Cookie said defensively.

Shannon smiled. "It does have an odor, but it'll help your face heal."

Molly nodded. "Does it really matter? I doubt I'll be here long enough for it to heal."

Everyone was silent and somber after that. The men finished eating then one by one, they nodded, and left.

"I'm sorry. I didn't mean for everyone to feel bad. Everything I do lately has been wrong. I apologize." Her heart broke. "It's almost Christmas, and here I am ruining it for every one of you."

Shannon stood up and sat in the empty chair next to Molly. "I'm sorry."

"It's not pity I'm after. You all had a life before me. A happy one without the problem of me. Don't worry I'll be fine." Molly did her best to smile. "Now where is this salve?"

Cookie smiled. "Coming right up." He brought over a big jar and when he opened it she almost gagged.

"People really use this?"

"Smart people do," Cooke responded. "Here let me help you put it on."

She silently prayed the whole time and then some afterwards. The smell didn't go away. "I'm going back to the cabin. Poor Boy, you don't have to come. I promise I won't run away."

His lips twitched. "I can stand it if you can."

"We could finish decorating the tree. Christmas will be here in two days." She brightened for his sake.

"Let's get it done—alone this time. We don't need help."

"No, we don't."

"See you two back for lunch," Cookie called as they went out the front door.

She dreaded coming back and having the men stare at her, but she hadn't done anything wrong. She had every right to hold her head up high…this time at least. She walked with

Poor Boy to the cabin, and her confidence wilted with each step. This was a problem of her own making.

POOR BOY strung popcorn and hung the strings on the highest branches while Molly did the bottom half of the tree. He tried his best to entangle them, and they laughed as they tried to untangle themselves. Her laughter was a beautiful, light sound. It was almost musical and his heart lightened.

The future was too unknown, but he hoped they'd be able have a nice Christmas together. It would be the memories he'd live off on when she was gone. A chill ran the length of his spine. His thoughts shouldn't have gone there, the lightness he felt darkened considerably. Why Molly? Why'd he have to fall for her? There was no future. He took a deep breath and slowly let it out. They had today and hopefully tomorrow and if he wanted happy memories, he'd better make some happiness.

He took her hand and then took a giant step back from the tree. "Looks good, doesn't it?"

She nodded. "It sure does. I do believe it's the biggest tree I've ever had. Thank you, Poor Boy. You've gone out of your way to make me forget, and I appreciate it more than you know." She turned. Stood up on tipped toe and kissed his cheek. "Ouch. I guess I shouldn't have done that."

"Since it hurt you maybe not, but I liked it all the same. You are unlike anyone I've ever known. It's hard to explain, but I feel as though I've known you since forever. You're straightforward. And you don't hide your feelings. Well, not very well anyway."

"I've always been an awful liar. People can tell by my face if I try, so I don't bother. One lie leads to another and then another, and before you know it, they all tumble down on you. We had to lie about ourselves everywhere we went, and I was mostly kept out of sight. My family was always afraid I'd give them away. They were probably right. Thank you for doing the holiday with me. You could have easily just sat there and treated me like a prisoner. I feel a connection to you too. Strange as it is, I'm comfortable around you."

His heart swelled with love and hurt all at the same time. They might have a day or two left.

"Will Edith expect you to spend Christmas with her? She seems to have adopted you in a way."

"I hadn't given it much thought. I figured she'd be out here with Cookie. I suppose it's better to find out what the plans are. I just don't know about her. She's the nicest to me, but the way she treated you is just plain wrong."

Molly touched his arm. "Listen, she'll be here long after I'm gone. Don't cut ties for me. Just let it go for now. From when I gather she thinks you and Anne Marie are suited."

He half chuckled. "That is not going to happen. If there is one thing I've learned, it's if a woman flutters her eyelashes too much she's up to something. Ann Marie was all about fluttering and when that didn't work, she said she had some-thing in her eye and asked me to look. I moved closer and she wrapped her arms around my neck and tried to give me a kiss. She's strong. It took a lot to get her off of me."

"Sounds to me like she expects you to be her husband. Who knows what Edith told her. Anyway, let's not think about them now. Do you know any Christmas Carols?"

"You want me to sing?" His face heated.

"Surely you know some and yes I want you to sing." Her eyes were full of humor.

"If we both sing it'll be fine I suppose." Singing wasn't something he did but for her he would. They sang "Silent Night" and "Joy to the World" then "Hark! The Herald Angels Sing" and "It Came Upon a Midnight Clear". Poor Boy didn't know all the words so he made some up. Soon enough they were laughing.

Lunchtime approached, and the singing stopped. She looked forlorn, and he wanted to make things easier for her.

"I'll go down to the main house and grab some grub. We can have a picnic in front of the tree." He knew she was pleased by the relief in her eyes.

"Thank you."

He grabbed his hat and coat and walked outside.

———

THE NEXT MORNING AFTER BREAKFAST, Cookie broke the bad news that Judge Gleason was in town. Molly's heart pounded out of control at Cookie's words. The blood drained from her face, and the room began to spin. Poor Boy caught her by the elbow and guided her to the settee.

"Any word when he'll be out here?" Cinders asked.

"Any time now, from what I heard," Cookie said.

Shannon sat down with baby Robert on her lap. "Judge Gleason is a fair man, Molly. We have to hope for the best."

"Will he take me today?" Tears rolled down her face.

"I honestly don't know with tomorrow being Christmas Eve and all. He may let you stay here or take you back to town, I just don't know."

"Or he might hang me." She dashed away her tears and it took all her strength to hold herself together. "I shouldn't have said that. It's the holidays, and my problems are my own. I don't want to ruin your happiness. It's a situation of my own making."

Robert began to squirm and reached for Molly, and she readily took him. What a delight. Shannon and Cinders were truly blessed. They seemed to know it too. What they had was rare, and it was what she would have wanted. But she'd also had a rare couple of days with an amazing man. She hugged Robert to her and then handed him back to Shannon.

Suppressing a sigh, Molly stood and went to Poor Boy, put her arms around his middle, and leaned against him. He returned her embrace and held her to him. She'd be gone but he'd be left behind. "I need to talk to you."

He nodded and led her outside.

As he started toward the cabin, she pulled him to a stop. "I want to spend as much time outside as I can."

Poor Boy turned toward her and gazed into her eyes. "Everything will be fine."

"You don't know that. I came out here to say a few things while I can." He started to interrupt, but she put her hand up and shook her head. "Let me say this while I can. I'm trying to be brave, but we both know I'm not. So, here goes. I've never met anyone like you before. You are the best man I've ever met. Somehow, you've gotten beyond every barrier I've put up and you are in my heart. You fill my heart. I already know what the judge is obligated to do. But I'm not sorry I fell in love with you. It's been the very best part of my life. When I'm gone, though, you need to go on. You have so much to give, and you deserve a loving wife and family. Don't settle for anything less than love, but don't avoid it. There's someone out there for you. Not Ann Marie, mind you, but someone sweet and loving. I wish beautiful sunrises and peaceful sunsets for you Poor Boy. I wish for you to walk in the light and never the darkness. Can you do that for me?"

She took a deep steadying breath before she dared to look into his eyes. She shouldn't have looked. His eyes were filled with tears. Her heart skipped a beat as she tried to hold herself together.

"I love you too. You've been the best part of my life too. I'll fight for you as much as I can. I'll talk to Shane and Judge Gleason. There has to be another answer."

There wasn't, and she knew it, but she nodded anyway for his sake. "Perhaps you're right. People talk about Christmas miracles. I've never put much stock in it, but maybe."

The sound of a wagon approaching made her heart drop. This was it.

CHAPTER SEVEN

Shane drove the wagon with Judge Gleason by his side. "Whoa," Shane said as he stopped the horses. Shane nodded to both Molly and Poor Boy. Then he tied off the reins. He jumped down and waited for the judge to climb off.

Poor Boy automatically reached and took Molly's hand in his. "Shane, Judge Gleason, good to see you."

"Well, look at you, son. You're a man now. You've been missed around Asherville. I'm darn glad to see you back."

"Thank you, sir."

"I take it this is the prisoner?" He pointedly stared at their joined hands.

Molly let go of Poor Boy's hand and stepped forward. "I am, your honor. I'm the one you're here to hang."

A lump formed in Poor Boy's neck. She was so very brave. Others might have cut and run, but not Molly.

"I guess that's what I'm here to determine," the judge said solemnly. "Let's get out of the cold. I hope Cookie has something sweet to eat. I'm in the mood for cookies or a cake." He led the way into the main house.

How could the judge could talk about food when all Poor Boy wanted to do was throw up? Nothing made sense any more. They all went into the main house and Cinders, Shannon, and Cookie all welcomed them.

They sat around the big dining table. Cookie quickly had coffee made and set out cookies he'd made earlier before he sat down to join them. Poor Boy could feel the tension in the room. He was wound up tight waiting for Judge Gleason to say something. The fear in Molly's eyes had him wishing he could just take her and run.

Judge Gleason ran his fingers through his white hair, which hung below his collar. He never looked much like a conventional judge. He always wore a crisp white shirt with black pants, but he looked and acted like the rest of the town folks. "What we have is a dilemma. Yes indeed." He stared at Molly, seeming to take her measure. "I'm not quite sure what to do with you, miss. On one hand you look to be decent enough, but on the other hand there was that bank robbery." He sighed.

"But—"Shannon started.

"No, no interruptions please. Here's the deal. We don't take bank robbing lightly, and we can't send out a message that we immediately forgive those who rob us at gunpoint. There are a few in town who want a hanging. There are a few hankering for a trial. What do you think, Deputy?"

Poor Boy startled. "She's been a model prisoner, sir. I have found her to be a kind, caring woman."

The judge nodded and gazed at Cinders. "Hear tell, you have them living in the same cabin here. That plain isn't good for anyone's reputation. How are people supposed to think of Poor Boy as a deputy when he lives with the prisoner? I leave town, and all heck breaks loose. I'm sorry, miss, but you need to come back to town and spend some time in the jailhouse while I look into this some more."

"We're not exactly equipped to house a female at the jail," Shane explained. "That's one of the reasons she's out here. That and the line of bounty hunters who have been by the office sniffing around."

"I understand but the people in town, the ones out for blood, don't understand. Personally, I would have found another option, one that doesn't include the deputy living with his prisoner. Cinders, I made you marry Shannon so she wouldn't be a single female living in this house with you. All right, grab your things and we'll head back to town." His tone announced he would tolerate no debate. He swigged his coffee down, put his hat on his head, and went out the door.

Molly's eyes grew wide. "What just happened? Am I going to hang or not?"

Shannon reached across the table and patted Molly's hand. "That's the thing. He didn't say. You go on to town, and Cinders and I will gather reinforcements to come to town."

Molly nodded and stood. "Poor Boy, can I go and get my things?"

"We don't want to make the judge mad. Cinders you'll bring our things to town, won't you?"

"Sure thing. Everything will be fine. I'll round up Tramp and Keegan, and we'll meet you in town."

Tears fell from Molly's eyes. "I don't know how to thank you."

Shannon's eyes also glistened. "We'll see you soon."

Poor Boy took Molly's hand and entwined his fingers with hers. "We might as well go."

Her brave smile was a bit wobbly and it had him loving her all the more. He helped her into the back of the wagon as he swung up on the horse Rollo had ready for him. He'd known it was coming, but it was much harder than he thought.

Her stomach churned with the rocking of the wagon. The ride back to town seemed shorter somehow. She'd expected the street to be lined with angry citizens, but instead it was only Edith and Aaron who stood and watched her go into the jail. Not knowing what to expect, she began to shake, and when Cecily stepped forward to hug her, it was most welcome.

"You'll be fine," Cecily whispered before she let her go. Her kind smile almost brought Molly to tears again.

Being brave was so very hard and she couldn't do it. She just couldn't. How she wished she could curl up and hide somewhere no one could ever find her. But she was an adult, and she didn't have the option of running away. Which was worse, pondering her fate or knowing her fate? She'd find out soon enough.

It was Christmas Eve tomorrow, and there was a very real possibility she wouldn't be around to see it. They led her to the same cell she had occupied before, handed her belongings to her and then Shane closed the door with a *clank*. It was a sound that echoed within her. With her back to them she took a few deep breaths to steady herself. She turned around and tried to hold her head up high. She wasn't certain if she really succeeded.

"Now what?" she asked.

"It's up to Judge Gleason," Shane told her.

She nodded, bit her bottom lip, and sat down. She'd done a lot of waiting the last few years. Waiting and praying her brothers would come home safe. How could an unjust accusation ruin her whole family? This time it wasn't unjust. She'd held a gun, and she robbed the bank.

Cinders and Shannon arrived with Tramp and Ilene. Molly smiled at them and nodded when they asked if she was all right. A big man with a pretty woman alongside him entered, and it was obvious the couple were good friends with the rest of the folks.

"Hi Molly, I'm Addy and this is my husband Keegan. We're so sorry to hear about your troubles. We hope we can help in some small way."

"Thank you." She sighed, not able to make small talk.

Keegan stepped forward and addressed the group. "First we need a place for her to live and a job. We don't want any objections on that level. Next, we make her out to be a good Christian woman."

"I *am* a Christian woman," Molly said.

Keegan nodded. "Down on her luck, forced by her father."

"I was certainly not forced by my father. There was another man who threatened us if we didn't pull the robbery for him. It wasn't the right thing to do, and I voiced my concerns over and over, but in the end we had no choice."

Keegan smiled broadly. "Good you do have some fight in you."

Molly frowned at them all until she locked gazes with Poor Boy. His concern for her was almost overwhelming. She changed her frown into a smile just for him. She noticed the exchanged looks between the others, but she didn't care.

"The man's name is Drew and he stayed at the saloon. I asked Noreen about him. Molly's story pans out," Poor Boy said.

Tramp cleared his voice. "We have all we need to know, I believe. Let's go to the saloon."

The saloon? What was he talking about?

"Poor Boy, keep an eye on the prisoner," Shane said as he led the charge out the door.

"That's it? Now they go and have a drink?" Her hope shriveled inside her.

"Oh, Good Lord, no. It's not what you think," Ilene

quickly replied. "The judge hangs out at the saloon most days. He's a tea teetotaler but he believes he's most effective where the people are."

"I see," Molly said but she didn't have a clue what was going on.

"He eats breakfast at Eats' every morning so the women can see him then," Addy added.

Looking down at her lap, Molly pretended to smooth out wrinkles on her skirt. She couldn't stand to have them all stare at her. The door opened, and she quickly looked up. Edith had arrived.

"Back where you belong. Good." She turned to Shannon. "Did Cookie come to town?"

"No, he volunteered to watch the kids."

"Mine too," Addy said.

"You left your children to come here for her?" She raised her hand and pointed at Molly.

"Isn't that what friends do?" Shannon asked.

Edith's brow furrowed. "I'm just glad she's behind bars. I expect you all will be attending the Christmas Eve festivities at the church tomorrow. We really need a preacher of our own. Ever since Pastor Sands died, all we've had is that circuit preacher, and he's not due here until after the winter."

"I'm sure we can pray just as well on our own," Cecily said. "It'll just be nice to have the community together."

"When's the hanging? Tonight would be best or we'll have to wait until after Christmas."

Poor Boy put his arm around Edith's shoulder. "Now, none of that talk around here."

Edith glared at Molly. "Fine, I have food to prepare for tomorrow night. Ann Marie will be there."

Poor Boy escorted Edith out the door. He must have walked her home, because he came back a few minutes later and gave Molly an apologetic grin. "Don't worry about her. She's the same way with most folks around here."

Molly nodded to him.

"Well, we brought your things. It looks like you'll be sleeping here tonight. But I promise you we will have our say at Eats' tomorrow morning. The men are laying the groundwork tonight, and we will do our best to get you set free." Shannon then gave Poor Boy a hug. "Hang in there."

Minutes later, Molly was alone with Poor Boy. "Maybe Edith is right. They might still come for me tonight. Who's going to allow a bank robber to ruin the town's Christmas?"

"Don't get ahead of yourself. Judge Gleason is a fair man. I don't know what the outcome will be, and to tell you the truth Molly I'm as afraid as you. I'm afraid that I've finally found love, and I might lose it. My home is wherever you are, and if something was to happen and they take you away, I don't know how I'd survive." The tears in his eyes broke her heart.

"I feel the same way. We just found each other and now…I can't find the right words to express how much I'm grieving already."

"Exactly, I feel like I'm already grieving and my heart is being ripped out of my chest."

Shane walked in, and she didn't even bother to wipe her eyes. It was too much.

"I know this is hard, but things will look better in the morning. The judge is a hardheaded man at times, but he has his own ways. He said he'd think on it and let us know in the morning."

Poor Boy's Adam's apple bobbed as he swallowed hard. "In the morning then."

"I'll be back at sunrise. We gave it our best shot, and I'm hoping for the best outcome." Shane turned and left, but not before she saw the shimmer of moisture in his eyes.

"I'm so tired, but I don't want to sleep the last of my hours away."

"I know what you mean," Poor Boy agreed. He grabbed two tin mugs from a wooden shelf and poured coffee into them. He handed one cup to her and while holding the other cup, he pulled a chair up to the bars. He reached through so they could hold hands.

Hours later, Molly watched Poor Boy sleep. They'd stayed awake most of the night, but finally he had nodded off. He looked so very young, and she wondered if that was the boy everyone remembered. To her, he was her hero. A man of integrity and kindness. A man with so much love to give. She shook her head. She'd cried too much already. She didn't want him to remember her with red eyes and nose. Instead, she took down her hair, unbraided it, and then brushed it. There was no sense going to the gallows looking shabby. She rebraided her hair and left it hanging down her back.

Then dawn was upon them, and she was afraid she wouldn't get a chance to talk to Poor Boy again. And yet... while he slept, he felt no pain. His anguish mirrored hers, and she didn't wish that for him.

The door opened and Poor Boy woke. Judge Gleason popped his head in. "Poor Boy I'd like to talk to you. Come on I'll buy you breakfast."

Poor Boy stood and gave her one last long look before he left.

CHAPTER EIGHT

*J*udge Gleason led the way to Eats' Place. Ann Marie gave him the same smile she had given Poor Boy a few nights ago.

"It's nice to see you both. Would you like your usual table, Judge Gleason? I'm sure you have details of the hanging to talk over. I'm glad you're here to protect the good citizens of Asherville." She waited until she was behind the judge before she glared at Poor Boy. "I'll get you both some coffee."

"She's a chipper little thing, don't you think?" Judge Gleason asked.

"If you say so."

"Don't care for her much, do you?"

"I don't really care for either of the Pikes. Aaron beat Molly the other night."

"Ahh, yes, I heard." Judge Gleason shook his head. "Something not quite right about him, I think."

Ann Marie returned with the coffee and set it down. "Judge, would you like the usual?" She waited for a nod. "What can I get you, Poor Boy? The steak and biscuits are always a favorite."

"That'll be fine." He waited until she walked away. "Have you made a decision about Molly?"

"I've mulled the problem over a few times. There seems to be a lot to take into consideration. Now it wouldn't be right for her to just ride out of town. Armed robbery coerced or not is a serious matter. She did lose her father, but that's what happens when you commit crimes. This is serious business. The man named, Drew was never found. And I did hear about the attack on her by Aaron Pike. Never did like him. I heard that everyone and their wives like her. It seems she's good with children too. Now I want to hear your opinion of her."

Poor Boy's jaw dropped for a brief moment. What if he said the wrong thing? "She came willingly into custody. I have to say she's been a model prisoner. She does what she's told."

Judge Gleason shook his head. "No. I don't want to know about her as a prisoner. I want to know her as a person."

Ann Marie placed their plates in front of them and left, giving Poor Boy a moment to gather his thoughts.

"She's one of the nicest girls I know. She's a real person. What I mean is, she doesn't put on airs. She's herself, and she's easy to talk to. She never wanted a life of crime. She's the planting roots type of person. Her brother was falsely accused of murder, and the whole family went on the run. They pulled a few robberies to survive. Molly never took part until the last one. All her brothers were dead, and she didn't want her father to go alone. There is a kindness in her I've never known before. She even has a smile on her face when she wakes up. Now, you have to agree that's rare. Her smiles are full of sunshine, and her heart is good."

Judge Gleason grinned. "So you like her."

"Yes sir, I do."

The judge nodded. "I ate while you talked. Finish up. I

have some things to take care of I'll see you tonight at the party." He hurried off before Poor Boy had a chance to ask any questions.

"Is the hanging going to be tonight?" Ann Marie asked as she began to clear dishes off the table.

Poor Boy threw down his napkin on the table, stood and walked away without answering her. He walked outside along the boardwalk, wondering what was going on. He'd have to find out from Shane if there was a women's prison in the area. It didn't sound as though hanging was in her future, but he was certain Judge Gleason had already made up his mind about something.

He walked by the church and saw all the people helping to decorate it. They were setting the pews around the outer edges of the room to make room for the celebration. He hadn't planned on going but Judge Gleason had made it sound as though he was supposed to be there. He wasn't much in the mood. He didn't know anything other than Molly wouldn't be hanging from a rope today. His jaw clenched and the tension in his shoulders wouldn't go away.

Facing Molly wasn't going to be easy. He didn't know what to say to her. If only they'd met under different circumstances. With a heavy heart, he went back to the jail.

———

MOLLY SMILED AT POOR BOY. "Whatever happens, we have now. I'm tired of thinking about the future. I'm sick of being scared and feeling like my heart is being ripped out of me. You're my heart, and we are here together. Pull the chair closer so we can hold hands. I feel better when you are near." She tried to sound as cheerful as she could. She'd be dead but he'd be left to suffer and the suffering didn't have to start right now. Not when they still had time.

They sat facing each other with the bars between them, holding hands. "Tell me what you like to eat on Christmas. Do you like pies or cookies best? What part of the turkey is your favorite?"

He chuckled. "Curious, aren't you? I like whatever is being served but I have to say the dressing is my favorite. For the holidays, I prefer pies. Pumpkin and apple are my favorites. Cookies are good, but I can have them year round. The turkey leg is my favorite. It always has been. Eats used to make turkey on Christmas for those who had no place to go. We had a lot of fun. He always gave me two oranges and a handful of candy. He tried to tell me Santa Claus brought me shoes and clothes but I never believed him. He was a good man. I miss him. When I was in New York, the schoolmaster's wife made dinner for those of us who were left behind. We had to dress nicely, and if you didn't use your good manners, the schoolmaster whacked your hand with a ruler. The food was good, but it wasn't fun."

"My father used to whittle, and he could make anything. He made animals the most. I had a collection of them. Let's see, there was a bear, a duck, a horse, a beaver. One time he carved me an Indian. I had a special box I kept them in. I'd help my Ma make dinner. We'd always joke that it took hours and hours to make but only a quarter hour to eat. I miss my family a lot but I can't look back and I refuse to look forward. Did you sing Christmas Carols?"

"You got me there. Except for the other night with you, I always pretended to sing. I'd just move my lips. I used to be too shy to sing in public I guess. You haven't asked what the judge had to say."

She nodded. "I know. If he'd let me go, you would have opened the cell door already. We'll know when we know." A strange calmness engulfed her, a sense of everything would be fine. If only the feeling would last. "Have you ever made a snowman?" she asked, changing the subject. "How about had a snowball fight?"

"There was one winter where we got enough snow for a snowball fight. Not so much to build a big snowman though. Lots of kids made them in New York, but we weren't allowed to."

She furrowed her brow. "Sounds as though you didn't have much fun at school."

He shrugged. "I was a good student, which surprised me. I worked hard. I had a few friends but no, there wasn't much fun there. I'm grateful for the education, and that was all Edith's doing."

They paused and stared at each other for a while. It was comfortable to sit with Poor Boy.

Shane came into the jailhouse. "Poor Boy, you're needed at my house. I'll watch Molly for a bit."

Poor Boy nodded and gave her a sad smile as though he'd never see her again.

She smiled at him. "I'll see you soon." She watched him walk out the door. She wrapped her arms around her waist to ward off the sudden chill.

"Don't look so glum," Shane said. He's going to my house to get dressed for the party. Cecily will be here in a few minutes to get you ready."

Fear clutched her heart. "Get me ready for what?" She took a deep breath and waited for him to tell her it was for the hanging.

"The Christmas party. Judge Gleason has orders for the two of you to show up. Cecily is bringing a dress for you. I really don't know what is going on inside the judge's head, but if he wants you at the party, at the party you will be."

"It's at the church isn't it? So, it can't be something too bad. Maybe he's giving me a respite until after Christmas."

Her mind whirled with possibilities and none of them ended well.

"I see the women coming this way now. I'll take my leave. I'll be back to escort you to the church."

Molly nodded, too confused to say anything. She watched as Addy, Ilene, Shannon and Cecily all marched into the sheriff's office. Shane gave Cecily a quick kiss before he left.

Shannon lifted a dress out of the basket she carried. "I didn't have much time, but I altered one of Addy's dresses for you to wear to the party." She pulled out a lilac colored dress with a white bodice. It was much fancier than anything Molly had ever worn before. "Let's get this on you and see if it needs to be fitted better."

Molly then noticed that the ladies were all dressed in their finest. She gazed at Addy. "Are you sure you want me to wear it? It looks too pretty for someone like me."

"I think it will be lovely on you," Addy answered as she used the key to open the cell door.

"Come on out," Ilene encouraged. "I'll fix your hair."

Molly walked out of the cell and felt suddenly shy. It was hard to believe that these wonderful women were taking her under their wings. They all began to help her undress and before she could protest, the new dress was placed on her.

They took a step back and stared at her. Shannon took a step forward and straightened the full skirt. "It's lovely on you. I have some face powder to hide those marks Aaron put on your face. And Cecily is letting you borrow her fancy blue dress coat to complete the outfit."

They sat her down and Shannon lightly put the powder on her face while Ilene brushed out her hair. Ilene pulled it back and fastened it so much of it hung down.

"I don't know what to say. Did the judge give you any reason as to why I'm to appear at the party?"

"Gleason can be a bit eccentric, and right now it's anyone's guess," Ilene told her. "It's time to go."

Cecily looked out the window. "You're right. Shane should be here any minute. She smiled at Molly. "You are a picture of loveliness."

Molly's heart was lifted up by her friends. She'd never known women like these. It was a treat to be part of their group.

"Ladies, Shane is coming down the walk," Shannon announced.

They all put their wraps on to ward off the cold. And one by one they left the jailhouse. Shane put out two elbows in order to escort both Cecily and Molly to the party. It was a short, cold walk and they were happy when they were inside the church. It was filled with people but the only person Molly saw was Poor Boy.

He wore a new plaid shirt, and he looked so very handsome, her chest tightened, making it difficult to draw a breath. When he turned and saw her the awe in his eyes melted her. All conversation faded into the background, and it was as though they were the only two people in the room. They gravitated toward the center of the room, until they met, standing toe to toe, staring into each other's eyes.

"I've never seen a more beautiful woman," Poor Boy said.

"You clean up real nice yourself," Molly replied. She was afraid to move, afraid to look away lest the moment disappeared.

"I still don't know why we've been summoned to this party." Poor Boy gave her a half grin. They wouldn't be able to enjoy the evening if they didn't know what was going on.

Molly hadn't noticed the whispers and stares at first, but she soon became aware of them. She wanted to leave, but she wasn't allowed. She saw Edith hurrying toward them and cringed. But before Edith got there, Judge Gleason was by their side.

Molly began to tremble. Ann Marie and Aaron soon joined Edith, and they all stopped right in front of her.

"I don't believe she's on the guest list," Edith said as she put her hands on her hips.

Ann Marie nodded in agreement while Aaron gave her a sneer.

Judge Gleason took a step forward. "I wasn't aware there was a list. It's a party for the whole town."

"She isn't part of the town," Edith insisted.

The judge turned and faced Molly and Poor Boy. "Dearly beloved."

Molly grabbed onto Poor Boy's hand. What was happening? She barely heard the words Judge Gleason was saying but she knew enough to know they were wedding vows. She glanced at Poor Boy, and he seemed to be in as much shock as her. She must have made all the proper responses because the next thing she knew, Poor Boy was giving her a kiss.

Poor Boy was kissing her. His firm lips softened upon hers and her body hummed. It was a kiss of love, a kiss of promise, and a kiss of a future for them. He finally broke the kiss and smiled at her.

Most of the people at the party clapped for them with the distinct exception of Edith, Ann Marie, and Aaron. Edith's disapproval seemed to bother Poor Boy, and that saddened Molly.

"Maybe this isn't a good idea. You didn't get a say in the matter, and I know how much Edith means to you…"

"I could have objected at any time. But I didn't because I want to spend my life with you. I love you." He kissed her on the cheek. "It'll be fine. I would have done anything to keep you safe."

"I love you too, so very much. Now we can actually plan a future together."

"Judge Gleason," Edith called loudly. "What is the meaning of all this? She is a bank robber, and Poor Boy is promised to someone else."

Shannon stepped forward. "What do you mean he's promised to someone else? Did he know?"

"He's promised to Ann Marie. He took her for a nighttime stroll and everything." Edith's voice became louder with each word. "Isn't that right, Ann Marie?"

Ann Marie's face grew bright red but she didn't say a word.

"Why she could be carrying his baby, for all we know!" Aaron accused.

Judge Gleason raised his hands for silence. "Poor Boy, is she carrying your baby?"

"No sir, I don't see how it would be possible. She tried everything to get me to kiss her. But it isn't her I love."

"Aaron, you seem to me to be a man who will do or say anything to get your own way. After your behavior here today and the way you tried to force yourself on Molly a few evenings ago, I have to say I've lost all respect for you. There are extenuating circumstances. There is still the question of this man Drew. Also out of her need to survive and her loyalty to her father she'd become an accomplice in the robbery." Judge Gleason turned to Poor Boy and Molly. "If either of you don't want this arrangement, let me know. I just figured to keep Molly from hanging the best thing to do was to get you two married and settled."

Poor Boy stood up nice and tall. "I think I fell in love with Molly the moment I saw her. This is the most precious Christmas gift I could have received. I wasn't sure what I was going to do without her. I'm the happiest man alive this Christmas Eve. Thank you, sir."

"I love Poor Boy with all my heart, and I thank you for your decision, Judge Gleason."

"In that case, let's get back to celebrating," Shane suggested.

Dancing in Poor Boy's arms was a dream come true. Aaron and Ann Marie stormed off, but Molly didn't care. Miracles did happen at Christmas. They twirled and twirled around the dance floor until Poor Boy whispered in her ear he needed to talk to Edith. She nodded and let him go.

Poor Boy walked across the room and spoke to Edith for a while. It was nice to see her face change from being pinched to actually smiling. Molly was happy for Poor Boy. He really did care about Edith.

As soon as he finished with Edith, he walked across the church toward Molly, his eyes so filled with love, she wanted to cry big happy tears.

He stood in front of her and dried her tears with the pad of his thumb. A bright smile lifted his lips. "Merry Christmas, Mrs. Hastings. I love you with a forever kind of love."

"I love you too, Mr. Hastings."

EPILOGUE

*S*ix Months Later

POOR BOY finally finished judging the shooting contest at the Founder's' Day celebration. He glanced over and his heart overflowed to see Molly sitting under a tree surrounded by friends. Her smile was one of joy as she placed both hands on her burgeoning stomach. He was both thrilled and terrified to become a father. He'd never had one of his own, but he figured he learned a lot from Eats about being part of a family.

Ilene sat right beside Molly; she too was carrying a baby. He'd never seen Tramp so solicitous before. He never left Ilene's side it seemed. He walked over to where they all sat: Shannon, Cinders, Addy, Keegan, Cecily with her newest daughter Amy, Shane, Ilene, Tramp, and Molly. Pride swelled in his chest as he took a spot beside his beautiful wife.

It was a day the Lord had made. It was an afternoon full of sunshine and laughter. The adults watched the children all play, while they talked about the changes in the town over the last few months.

Soon after Christmas, Poor Boy had fired both Ann Marie and Aaron. Edith backed him in his decision, and it felt good to have her on his side. For a while, Molly had run the restaurant while he continued to work as deputy. It had been hard, but they made it work. But the moment Molly told him she was with child, he hired a few widows to take over.

Both he and Shane were constantly looking for leads on the man who held a gun on Molly and her father during the bank robbery. Molly never did get a good look at him so the clues were sparse.

He and Molly bought land next to Shane's place, and with Cecily's help, they now had a garden and some livestock. There was enough land to raise cattle on, and Poor Boy planned to do that next. He walked to where they all sat. He noticed a few of the wives were whispering when Edith approached carrying something under her arm.

"Every year the quilting group of Asherville makes a quilt to give to a resident on Founders' Day. This year we pick you, Poor Boy...you and Molly." She unfolded the quilt and everyone commented on its beauty.

"The one for next year goes to me and Cookie. We're finally going to get married in September. You are all invited!"

Cinders was the first to stand and give her a kiss. "Where is Cookie?"

"He decided to judge the pie baking contest. Since Ilene didn't enter this year, he is taking it upon himself to make sure someone is worthy of first prize."

"Where are you going to live?" Tramp asked.

"We're working on that part." She smiled from ear to ear.

"Thank you all so much for the beautiful quilt. I wish I

knew how to sew," Molly said, her voice filled with wistfulness.

"Join the quilting circle. We can show you," Edith said.

Poor Boy and Molly were the last to hug and kiss Edith. After that, Poor Boy took Molly's hand and led her into a grove of trees. As soon as they were out of sight, he pulled her into his arms and kissed her. The way she eagerly kissed him back always made him feel ten feet tall. He held her against him and gave silent heartfelt thanks to God for always looking out for him and for guiding him to Molly. This past Christmas had held so much joy for him. Every time he looked at Molly, he was reminded of the special miracle he had received.

"I love you," she whispered in his ear.

He laughed. "I'm going to show you just how much I love you right now."

"Outside? Here?" Her eyes grew wide, then they filled with desire.

"This type of lovin' can't wait." He kissed her neck and reveled in the way she shivered.

"I agree it is something that seems rather urgent."

"Have I told you just how much I love you?" he asked.

"Yes, but now you can show me too."

THE END

I'm so pleased you chose to read Poor Boy's Christmas, and it's my sincere hope that you enjoyed the story. I would appreciate if you'd consider posting a review. This can help an author tremendously in obtaining a readership. My many thanks. ~ Kathleen

THE GREATEST GIFT

CHAPTER ONE

oster O'Donnell woke to total stillness, the silence of his world blanketed in snow. Throwing off his covers, he placed his feet on the cold wood floor and grimaced. He quickly dressed. He shook his head at his calico cat, Patches. "Staying in bed? Can't say that I blame you." Usually he kept cats in the barn to kill the mice, but Patches was a special case. Being the smallest of the litter, she got pushed aside until she lay alone, starving. From that moment on, he made sure Patches got her fair share.

He walked through the great room. The old hand-honed wooden cabin was freezing. He was grateful for the second-hand black and rusted wood stove. It heated the house fairly well. He stoked the banked embers and threw in some kindling to start the fire. Finally, it was burning enough for some bigger pieces of wood.

Throwing on his coat, boots and hat, he grabbed his lantern and headed out to the barn. His horses came first. They were his future. He'd invested everything into catching and breeding the mustangs, and he hoped for many more offspring.

A loud wrenching scream rang through the air. Startled, Foster raced to the barn. He opened the door and there on a mound of fresh hay lay a pretty little thing with red hair and blue eyes. Suddenly she grabbed her stomach and screamed again.

"Oh no, you're not having any baby here in my barn."

"Oh, thank God. Help me to your house please." She stared at him with pain and fear in her eyes.

"No."

"Look, like it or not this little one is coming into the world. I need you. I'm Ginger Galway." Tears filled her eyes.

"It's almost Christmas. Where's your family?"

She glanced away. "This baby is my family."

Ginger screamed again and he couldn't take it. Bending down, he scooped her into his arms, amazed how little she weighed. He quickly carried her into the cabin and laid her on his bed. "I'll put on water to heat and then help you."

"You've delivered babies?" Her eyes pleaded with him to say yes.

"No just foals, oh and a few kittens."

"Horses?"

"Yes, ma'am. I'm Foster O'Donnell."

"No you're not. Who are you? Foster is the father. I know that good-for-nothing skunk Foster O'Donnell, and it isn't you. Though why'd you want to be that low life—" She doubled over. "It hurts."

He hadn't a clue what she meant. She was babbling about another Foster? Maybe giving birth did something to a woman's brain. "Is this your first child?"

"Look at me, I'm barely out of school. Of course, it's my first child. I know, I know many girls get married right out of school, but I wanted to leave my hometown. I planned to be a teacher. I got my certificate and everything. But my aunt insisted I visit her in Chicago and that snake Foster came sniffing around, and I fell for all his lies. To my mortification and ever living shame I believed him."

"So you're Mrs. O'Donnell?" he asked as he took off her shoes.

She bit her lip and turned her head before she screamed in pain again. "No," she gasped. "I already told you my name is Ginger Galway. What are you doing?"

"I need to get most of your clothes off so the baby can come."

Her eyes narrowed. "It better be all you're doing."

Foster stood up straight and put his hands on his hips. "I have no desire seeing a woman in pain. I know we don't know each other but there will be parts of you I will have to see. I know it's awkward and downright embarrassing, but I don't see any other choice."

"Why aren't you married?" She looked him up and down. "Is there something wrong with you?"

Her words stung. "I was almost married once. Patty was her name. She liked me well enough, I guess, but didn't like the ranch. She knew I had a horse ranch but she expected bigger and better. She called my place a hovel." He put twine, a knife and some cloths into the boiling water.

"A hovel? She should see where I lived. Some people just don't know how to be grateful for what they have. When I first found myself with child, I bemoaned my circumstances, but this is a miracle given to me by God to care for. It hasn't been easy, especially wandering around these last few days, but you found me." She screamed in pain. Perspiration formed on her brow, and he took a clean cloth and wiped it away. She grabbed his hand and squeezed it as she screamed again.

Patches jumped on the bed, took one look at Ginger, hissed, and jumped back down.

"What was that?" She squeezed his hand harder.

"That's Patches, my cat."

"Oh."

Damn she was a strong one. He waited for the contraction to subside before he gently took his hand back. "The time is nearing." He took out the cloths from the water and laid them on the table he'd just cleaned. Next he got the knife and twine out of the water. He put the kettle on the table as well. He next poured some cold water into a pot. He wasn't sure how much she'd bleed but he knew the child would need to be cleaned. "I'm going to have to lift up your dress and see if the baby is starting to come out. This is no time for modesty." He stared into her blue eyes.

She nodded with tears in her eyes. "I understand. I wish you'd tell me your real name."

"Ma'am, my real name is Foster. I have a good idea who you met up with, though. I have a brother; we took different paths in life. This sounds like his doing." The baby was crowning. "Just a few more pushes, ma'am."

"My name is Ginger," she gasped between each word.

"Ginger, push hard when the pain comes again. I'm hoping to get a shoulder out. It's almost here! Push!" He grabbed the baby with a clean cloth. Quickly he tied off the umbilical cord and cut it with the sterile scissors. Gently he cleaned the baby and put it on Ginger's chest. "It's a girl. Hold her while I get you cleaned up."

Ginger gave him a dazed smile. "A girl! Imagine that." Tears ran down her face. "I'm glad I made a run for it. My pa would have put her out in the snow to freeze. He has no use for a girl. He told me so. If it was a boy he said he'd name him Foster so I'd remember my disgrace." She stroked the baby's head. "A redhead, good, maybe she won't look a thing like that, dang I don't even know his name."

"Albert, Albert O'Donnell. My brother from hell." He busied himself birthing the afterbirth and cleaning her. He knew the possibility of infection. He was always careful with his mares.

"He doesn't look like you."

"He wouldn't. My mother married his pa. There's no blood between us. Just a common name."

"Strange I ended up here and all. It's miracle I found anywhere to rest at all."

Foster put on his coat and grabbed the afterbirth, wrapped in towels. "I need to bury this. I'll be back." He closed the door behind him. A miracle? Perhaps a curse if it involved his brother. Ginger's family must have money or Albert wouldn't have bothered. His teeth chattered a bit as the wind blew stronger. Another snowstorm was headed his way. He'd have to tend to the horses later. In weather like this, they'd need the hay he bought for such an emergency. Getting it to them was the hard part. What was he going to do with Ginger and her baby? They certainly weren't his responsibility. She did have a point. Of all the possible places she could have ended up at, it was his ranch she came to.

Was her story even true? His brother asked to be part owner of the horse ranch when he saw it was making money. Not much but enough to buy hay. That was a few years back. Could be he was working with Ginger to get his ranch. His theory made more sense than her story.

A GIRL. Ginger's heart swelled as she stared at her daughter. Thank God, she found shelter. Foster, she had hated the name and the man. Her Foster didn't have wavy brown hair that hung to his shoulders or brown eyes with gold flecks in them. Nor did he have the look of a well-muscled man. Probably from all the ranch work. No, her Foster was blond, blue-eyed and compared to his brother a weakling. He was soft all over. A real sweet talker and she foolishly allowed him to talk her into his bed.

He proposed but asked her not to announce it. He was waiting for his family from New York to travel for the wedding and wanted to tell them in person. It mattered to him so she agreed. Her face heated as she thought of how easily he'd gotten her into his bed and tears of shame ran down her face. He laughed when she told him about the child. He actually laughed and left town the next day, leaving her to face her aunt, who, after slapping her face, promptly sent her home.

She took a deep breath and got ahold of herself. Today was a new day and she had a beautiful baby girl. It was hard but she sat up, placed the baby on her lap, and unwrapped her. What a darling girl. Her fingers and toes were so tiny. Her ears, her mouth everything was small and perfect. Her father had called her a sin and she'd half believed the child wouldn't be born right.

The frigid wind blew in as Foster came back inside. She quickly wrapped her baby and held her close. "Thank you," she said and quickly looked away. She'd always been shy and awkward until Fos—Albert.

"She seems healthy enough. I know you're tired but I need the truth from you. How long have you and Albert been planning this?" His voice was gritty with anger.

Her stomach clenched. He was getting ready to put her out. "Your brother ran out on me."

"So you came here expecting me to take responsibility for you and the baby?" He scowled.

"I'm so tired. I can't fight with you and I have a feeling whatever I say you'd think it wrong. I'm just asking to stay a few days until I'm healed up to go. It's my problem and I'll find the solution."

His brow furrowed and he nodded. At least she had a few days out of the winter cold.

"Of course. There's a better time for this talk. I'm sorry." He walked close to the bed and gazed down at the baby. "She sure is a pretty lass."

"Yes, she is." She yawned.

"You need to sleep. Go ahead I'll watch out for the wee one."

She opened her mouth to answer but promptly fell asleep.

She dreamt about a baby crying and a strong yet gentle voice trying to comfort the baby. It was such a peaceful feeling, she didn't want to wake up, but slowly she became alert enough to know her baby was crying and Foster was talking to her.

"You're awake," Foster said, his voice cheery and his face glowing faintly.

"I bet she's hungry. Will you hand her to me? How long did I sleep?" She sat up and held her arms out. They exchanged smiles as Foster put the baby in her arms.

"A few hours. She's a real sweetheart. I think she smiled at me. I know she waved at me. She seems to have taken a shine to Patches."

Ginger wanted to laugh but kept it to herself. No baby waved this early and there was no way she already liked the cat. "I'll feed her if you don't mind turning your back."

"I have to go and tend the horses. Some are a good distance from here, so don't be alarmed if I'm not back by nightfall. I left some bread and stew for you and I made a cradle. Well, it's really a crate, but I put a clean blanket in it." He grabbed his hat, coat, gloves and scarf before leaving.

"My sweet love, let me see if we can get this feeding figured out. I know it's supposed to be natural so let's try it." She untied the top of her chemise and let if fall. She took one arm then the other out of it and held the baby to her breast. As she suckled, she sighed in relief. "I promise to be the best mama I know how." She knew enough to change from one breast to the other.

While the baby suckled, Ginger glanced around Foster's home. It was cozy and warm. Whoever made it put time into it to be sure the winter wind didn't come through. There against one wall was the cook stove. All the kettles and skillets were placed in one crate near the stove. Patches lay in front of the stove napping. Tableware, a few tin cups, and plates graced shelves above the crate. A row of crates were hung vertically and held foodstuffs. She would have never thought to make shelves in that fashion. It was clever. There were pegs around the room. Some held clothes and there was a bridle hanging from one. The eating table had seen better days, but it too looked clean, and there were two chairs and two wooden stools.

The floor was made of wood and she stared at it. She'd only lived in places with dirt floors except for the time she lived in Chicago with her aunt. Her aunt had offered to make a match for her and she went to Chicago at her father's insistence. She was there for a long while until a few months after she met F-Albert. Goodness, it was hard to think of Albert as Albert and not Foster. She'd been sent home, disgraced. Back to the dirt floors.

Why her? Why out of all the socialites in Chicago did Albert pick her? She sighed. He knew she was plain stupid. It really was the only answer. Her father told her often enough she'd squandered her only chance for a good life. Tracing her fingers over her daughter's eyebrows, nose, and mouth, she shivered. Her father would have put the baby out in the snow, she had no doubt.

What to do? Where would they go? At least she had a couple days to figure it all out. She and the baby dozed on and off most of the day. Opening her eyes, the darkness surprised her. Slowly she got out of bed and lit a candle. There were two oil lamps but oil was too dear to use except for emergencies. Her stomach gurgled and she smiled. Foster's stew smelled wonderful and she was grateful for the chance to fill her belly again. It seemed like it'd been empty for far too long. Bending, she picked up a few small logs, threw them in the fire, and then helped herself to some dinner.

Her whole body ached and she was weak, but she was warm. It was a miracle her hands and feet weren't frost bitten. She'd thought for sure she'd lose a few toes. Closing her eyes, she thanked God. She'd been blessed her whole journey to the ranch. There were a few times she wanted to lie down and give up, but she plodded along in the bitter cold.

The door opened and Foster came in, stamping the snow off his boots. His gaze immediately went to the bed then he glanced her way and smiled. He was rather handsome when he smiled.

"I'll grab more wood," he said as his gaze lingered on her. Finally, he turned toward the door and went back outside.

She wished she was the reason for his smile, but they didn't know each other. He probably smiled because she was out of bed, meaning she would be able to leave fairly soon. They were an intrusion. When the baby began to fuss Ginger went to the bed and sat down; she uncovered her breasts and started to feed her daughter.

Foster entered with a pile of wood in his arms. He knelt and put it into a stack, while Patches jumped in and out of his way, then turned her way. Her heart thumped at the way Foster looked at her breasts. Raw desire leapt into his eyes before he glanced away.

Her face heated as her heart continued to thump. "I'm sorry. I should have covered up somehow."

"No, that's what mothers do, they feed their babies." He helped himself to dinner and sat at the table. "Have you named her yet?"

"No, I had so hoped it wasn't a girl. I refused to entertain the notion of a girl's name."

"You could name her after your mother."

"Molly. That is such a sweet name. You're right; I will name her after my mother. Molly O'Donnell."

"O'Donnell?" His brow furrowed.

Her heart sank. He didn't believe her. "Molly Galway it is. If she asks about her father I'll say I didn't know his name." She gave him her best glare.

"Oh, hell. You're right, O'Donnell is her birthright."

Her birthright? "I'll just call her Molly for now. It doesn't much matter. I don't plan to go home."

"Where are you planning to go?" He finished the last of his stew, crossed his arms across his strong chest, and stared at her.

"I don't know yet. I never got any further in my plan than to get here."

"Get here? So you did plan to come to my ranch the whole time." He scowled.

"Yes and no. Your brother told me this was his place, but I never imagined I'd get here. I headed for the nearby town but I must have missed it with all the snow falling. I didn't know whose barn I ended up in. I had hoped for a kindly woman."

"Albert sent you here, didn't he?"

"No. Like I said, he fled town when I told him I was carrying his babe. I suppose he found out I was a poor relation to my aunt. I don't know. I just knew I couldn't give birth at my father's farm. I was afraid for the baby."

"He wouldn't have put a girl child out to die."

A tear trickled down her face. "You don't know my father." She shifted on the bed, giving him a glimpse of her bare back. She heard his loud gasp and quickly turned again, this time grabbing a sheet to cover her and Molly.

"Damn his bloody soul!"

"That's what he said to me. It was my choice, which resulted in me carrying Albert's child. I did this and I was punished for it."

His eyebrow arched. "You believe the punishment was just?"

"The punishment yes, the way I was punished no," she whispered.

"Would you ever punish Molly like that?" he asked gently.

She couldn't look at him. "No, never. Thank you for helping me and I want you to know I'll be gone as soon as I'm able. I'm guessing in two days."

"Ginger, look at me." She gazed into his eyes and the kind understanding squeezed her heart. "It's Christmas in a week. Stay here and we won't have to celebrate alone."

She nodded but had no intention of imposing. In two days, she'd be fit to travel.

CHAPTER TWO

*T*wo days later, Foster gazed at his herd of horses. They were all accounted for and they looked well. The winter sky threatened yet another storm, and he hurriedly got as much hay to them as he could. They knew where their food came from at times like this, and he didn't have to go far to find them. Amazing majestic creatures, his horses were.

It had been bone-breaking work but he now had an Army contract for half his herd and most of those were saddle broke. A sense of pride ran through him. Things were looking good. The last few days had been a whirlwind of activity, but it made him realize just how alone he'd been. The best part was Ginger's smile and the look of wonderment and love she had whenever she gazed at Molly. Lucky girl was going to look just like her ma. Her red hair was already appearing. Hopefully she'd grow up without Albert's blood showing through. That shiftless lying bastard.

Ginger wasn't at his place by accident. He didn't buy that part of her story, but the rest rang true. He'd been gut kicked when he saw her back, full of scars. Some looked recent. How he wanted to strangle her father for putting his hands on her. It also scared him that he cared so much. He'd only met her and somehow she'd become important to him. His blood heated when he saw her. Her laughter was contagious and she was a kind and gentle mother.

He shook his head. It'd be best not to think of her that way. It would only lead him down the path of heartache. He finished emptying the sleigh of hay and turned Dancer around. Leading him on foot, they made their way home. He turned his collar up and wrapped the scarf over the lower half of his face. Yes, a storm was brewing, and it looked to be a bad one.

As they finally approached home, he saw lighted lamps. He chuckled. It had taken two days to convince her to use the lamps. She sure was frugal, a good trait for a wife. He swallowed hard. No more thinking about wives, she'd be gone soon.

After tending to Dancer's needs, Foster went inside. The warm cheerful atmosphere filled him. He'd never met a female who was happy before. The ones he'd come across always bemoaned their fate. Though he had to admit his mother had a right to be unhappy. Her husband was quick with his fists.

"Good, you're back. I have dinner ready for you," Ginger said as she flashed him a smile.

"You're going to spoil me." He took off his outer clothes and stretched his arms over his head. "The fierce cold tightens my muscles."

"Do you need me to help you?"

He grew hard thinking about it, but he shook his head. "No, a hot meal is all I need."

"You're easy to please." She spooned up some stew and set it on the table. "Come sit and eat."

He nodded but first walked over to the crate and gazed at Molly. She sure was a beauty. "How's she doing?"

"She's eating well, and sleeping well. I'm taking it as a good sign."

Foster nodded and sat at the table. "This smells good." He took a bite. "You're a good cook."

"My father never thought so."

"Either he's crazy or downright mean."

"Oh, I'd have to say he's both."

He laughed then sobered. "I'm sorry. It couldn't have been easy with a man like him."

She directed a sad smile his way. "I can't change what was, but I can change how I will raise my daughter. I will never raise a hand to her."

"I believe you. You're good with Molly." His heart pinged as she colored prettily.

"I'm trying to decide which direction to strike out tomorrow."

He frowned. "What do you mean?"

"I already told you I couldn't stay long. We're not your responsibility. Besides I bet you're anxious to have your peace and quiet back." She tried to look brave, but he saw how afraid she really was. She was right, he'd enjoyed his solitude, but having her and Molly around was nice.

"You won't be going far in the upcoming storm."

"Another storm? Walking through the snow isn't easy. As soon as the storm is over I'll be gone."

"Listen, Ginger, no rush." He wished he had more to say. A compelling reason why she shouldn't leave, but except for the storm all he had was she'd be safer, both she and the baby. "Christmas is in a few days, and I'd be honored to have you and Molly celebrate with me. I don't have much, but I hate being alone on Christmas." Patches meowed as if she echoed Foster's words.

She gazed into his eyes as though she was trying to read him. "Thank you for the offer. Are you a drinking man, Foster?"

He shrugged. "I've had a drink or two in my life. Usually I'm too busy to partake."

Again, she gazed into his eyes. "Holidays?"

"Why all the questions? I don't have anything in the house except for a bit of whiskey for emergencies. Medical emergencies. I'm not a drunk. I don't spend my money on liquor. If that's what you're used to then, I'm sorry for you."

She dropped her gaze and nodded. "I'd be delighted to stay until right after Christmas." Molly started fussing and Ginger hurried over to her. She cooed and sang to her as she fed her. This time he didn't look. Instead, he got up and cleared the table.

"I'll do that when I'm done here."

"No trouble. I'm used to doing it. You relax and take care of that beautiful child of yours." Her brow furrowed and she bit her bottom lip. He gave her what he hoped was a reassuring smile. "Not all men expect to be waited on."

"You'd be the first, Foster." She smiled. "See, I've stopped tripping over your name. I feel so stupid at how fooled I was by your brother. I knew he was a no-good rat, but I never thought he'd give me a fake name."

"He's probably on to another big city looking for another rich girl."

"I hope you're right."

GINGER WATCHED as Foster cleaned the dishes. He'd rolled up his sleeves and dark hair sprinkled his strong arms. So far, they had been protective and helpful arms. The thought of them around her made her shiver. At least he wasn't prone to drink himself to sleep each night. He was like no other man she'd ever known.

"What makes you so pensive? I hope you're not worried about the storm." Foster dried his hands with a towel and sat on a chair facing her. His dark hair had fallen boyishly across his forehead. He looked much younger that way.

"No, I guess I'm not smart enough to be worried about the dangers. You're different from other men."

He cocked his brow. "How so?"

"You have gone out of your way to take care of me. If I was home, I'd be expected to cook and clean."

"Even if you'd just given birth?"

"Yes. The stew you made was the first time a man had cooked my dinner. Well, I did go to a restaurant in Chicago and I don't know who cooked the meal but…"

"I know what you mean. I didn't know my real pa. Howard O'Donnell was the only pa I knew and he was the same way in his expectations. He worked my ma to death. He beat her and he sure knew how to make her cry. I promised myself I'd be a better man. I don't need to be like him, we have no blood in common." His brown eyes flashed with conviction. Her heart was already filled with love for Molly but whenever she looked at him, it seemed to want to expand to include him. She needed to guard her heart. No more men for her. Somehow, she'd make her own way.

"This really is a lovely cabin."

Foster nodded. "It took a long while to build. I lived in the barn for months. My horses' well-being comes first. They are going to help me make enough to have a great ranch. Maybe even a bigger house someday." He shrugged his shoulders. "I'm not looking to make it rich. I want a ranch to be proud of. Maybe even have a family someday. For now it's just me and Patches." He was quiet after that, as though he was lost in thought.

"Do you think the storm will be bad?" she asked, already knowing the answer. The quiet unnerved her.

"From how close to the house the horses are getting I'd say so. Don't worry, we'll be fine. I have enough chopped wood for three months at least, and I tied a rope from the cabin to the barn so no one will get lost in case of snow blindness."

Shivering, she wrapped her arms around her. "You have a reassuring manner, Foster. The type of man who's good in a crisis. I can shoot a gun, hunt, and ride. All out of necessity. Besides your brother, the only man I ever wanted to shoot was my father, but he's not worth getting strung up for."

"Impressive you can do all those things. When you went to live with your aunt, were you hoping to find a rich husband with servants?"

She laughed. "I'd shame any man by wanting to work side by side with the servants. My aunt dragged me out of the kitchen by my ear. She explained it wasn't my place to be there. It was terribly boring until Albert came along. He understood everything about me, or so I thought. You can add gullible to my list of traits." She frowned glumly.

"Hey we all get mixed up in things that seem great at the time. It's not your fault. The blame goes to Albert." She glanced away. There was no way she could look at him. He'd be sure to see the lies in her eyes. She needed to tell him the truth of how she found his cabin. She wasn't big on lies either.

"Foster—"

There was pounding on the door. Foster's brow furrowed and he grabbed his shotgun. "Who is it?" he yelled.

"Damn it, Foster, it's freezing out here!" Her heart sunk. She knew that voice, it was Albert. Fear and surprise shot through her. What was he doing here? Her stomach clenched as a huge lump formed in her throat. Instinctively she grabbed Molly and held her close.

Foster gave her an angry glare before he opened the door. "What do you want?"

"Foster, it's cold out here and a storm is a brewing. I thought I'd spend Christmas with you." He pushed past Foster and stomped into the cabin. His eyes lit with speculation when he spotted her and the baby. "I see you found the place. How long have you been here?"

"Found the place?" Foster shot her an angry, accusing glare. "I should have known. I have to hand it to you Miss Galway, you put on a fine performance. You really had me feeling bad for you."

"Foster—"

"Save it, Ginger. You have nothing to say I want to hear. If it wasn't snowing so bad I'd put you out." He turned toward Albert. "So, what's the plan? Get rid of me while you and your family take over my ranch?"

"We're not a family!" she insisted. The fury on Foster's face scared her. "I thought this was his ranch. He talked about it enough and told me how to get here. When my father threw me out, it was the only place I knew to go. Believe me, I didn't relish coming to the ranch of a man who threw me away, but I couldn't take the chance my father would put my baby out in the snow."

"You told her this was your ranch? What the hell is going on?"

Molly started to cry in earnest and nothing did comforted her. She wasn't hungry or wet.

"Can't you shut that brat up?" Albert sneered as he kicked at the cat.

"Look, you low-down lying snake, my daughter is not a brat, and we were just fine without you." She put Molly to her shoulder, lightly patting her back, but she still howled.

Foster shook his head and held out his arms. "I'll take her." His eyes gentled. She handed Molly to him and watched as he cradled her in his strong arms. Molly stared at him and sighed contently. She settled down and when he held her to his shoulder she promptly fell asleep.

"You're so good with her." Their gazes met, and she swore something connected between them.

"Here, let me hold the brat." Albert got close enough to Foster to start grabbing at Molly.

"Step away from me and Molly, Albert, or I swear to God I'll put you out. I really don't care if you freeze or not. I don't know what's going on around here, but I'm going to get to the bottom of all this deception."

Albert turned and pinned her with a beady stare. "You called her Molly? All the Mollys I know are lowly house servants. You don't have an ounce of class in you. If I weren't under the mistaken notion you came from money, I'd never have given you a second glance. You looked and acted like a poor, inferior relation. There isn't a regal bone in your body. I felt sorry for you, being so plain."

"That's enough, Albert. Ginger is a guest in my house and you will stop insulting her."

"Don't let her fool you, brother, she comes from trash. Her father is the town drunk. Said she was a virgin but there wasn't much blood after I took her."

Her face heated as tears welled in her eyes. She'd been a virgin. It was the only gift she had to give a husband. She'd tried so hard to learn everything her aunt taught her, from sitting properly to eating barely anything in front of company. She didn't know she was plain too. Being the town drunk's kid was bad enough. There were so many strikes against her.

"I think she's fetching, and you don't have to have money to have class. My mother said those words many times."

"Your mother was a used up piece—"

"I wouldn't if I were you," Foster warned as he gently set Molly into Ginger's arms. "I'm going to have to ask you to leave." His voice was deceptively calm.

"Fine, Ginger, get Molly ready to go." Albert smirked. "That child is mine, and I'm taking her with me."

"If that's what you want, Albert. I guess you're here to make good on your promise to marry me." She held her head high and looked him right in the eye. "Where will we live? Do you have a job lined up?"

He blanched. "A job?"

Her eyes narrowed. "Why are you here, Albert? You have a low opinion of me and you didn't want the baby. What game are you playing now?"

He stared at her for a long time then smiled. "The game we dreamed of, my sweet. The one where we take the ranch for ourselves. Why else would we be here? Is it my fault you're not playing your part? I guess you decided you'd rather have Foster than me."

She gasped. "Foster, open the door and push him out."

"Gladly, but I need to figure out what's going on around here."

HE KNEW his voice was rather sharp, but he didn't have it in him to be nice at the moment. He should have trusted his gut and never gotten to know Ginger. He'd become used to them being there, even if it had been a short time. He liked the way her eyes lit up when she saw him, or the special way Molly snuggled against his shoulder when he held her. They belonged to another and it made it even worse that it was Albert. How he hated the man. He always lorded it over him, he was the real son and Foster just an extra stray. The damned man he called father was just as bad, making Foster work from sun up to sundown while Albert went to school.

Albert had the best clothes while he wore cast offs. He didn't care at first. His mother seemed happy until the first time his father struck her. He ran all the way to town to get the sheriff but was instantly laughed out of the jailhouse. Somehow, his father already knew he'd gone to the sheriff. When he got home he got his first whipping while Albert watched, smirking.

"Albert, you've never done an honest day's work in your life. Don't bother looking for any money. I don't keep it here. I have it safe in the bank where you'll never get it. Don't even bother with the next of kin claim. You are of no blood of mine and I already had papers drawn up in the event of my death. So, you might as well go. I'd tell you to take your woman and child but the weather is getting worse."

Albert paled and turned toward Ginger. "Just how much did you tell him, my sweet?"

The anger on Ginger's face surprised him. "You no-good scoundrel. The only thing you ever told me was where the ranch was. A ranch I believed you owned, *Foster*. I will forever berate myself for being so stupid to believe you. You ruined my life when you ran away like the coward you are. My father threatened to put the baby out into the snow to die. Where did you go? Did you find another woman to shame?" Tears ran down her face and she tried to wipe them away but they kept coming.

"If you must know, I spent the last months with a wealthy widow. At least she knew how to please a man."

Foster stepped between them. "Not another word, Albert. It was bad enough you seduced her and left her, but the things you are saying will not be tolerated any longer. Understood?" It was getting harder not to punch him in the face. Perhaps Ginger was telling the truth after all. It made no real difference in the end. She couldn't be trusted either.

"I need to feed Molly. Please turn your backs." Her voice sounded small and wounded.

He turned around and grabbed a chair to sit in.

"Albert, please turn around."

"It's not like I haven't seen your large bosom before."

At her gasp, Foster turned, grabbed Albert by the back of his collar and dragged him to a chair facing away from Ginger. He pushed him down onto it. "Have some respect."

"I've—"

"If you don't shut your mouth I will gladly do it for you."

"You always were a ruffian. You'll never amount to anything. You and your few horses will keep you poor." Foster ignored the venom in his voice. A few horses? He was tempted to throw his Army contracts in his face, but somehow it would only make things worse.

"Meeting here was her idea, you know. Her daddy's place isn't more than a two days ride from here. It was all she could talk about after I told her about your ranch. She said she liked horses and taking over the ranch seemed like a good idea at the time. That was before I found out she spread her legs for any man."

Foster rose out of his chair and punched Albert's face. Blood gushed down the front of Albert's face and onto his shirt.

"You broke my nose! What kind of man are you?" Albert got up and grabbed a towel but not before he glanced over at Ginger. Patches sat on the bed next to her and Molly. She stood, arched her back and hissed at him. "Damn cat!"

"Your nose? Damn I was aiming for your jaw."

CHAPTER THREE

*S*leep evaded Ginger. She tossed and turned all night, fretting about her future. A future, which did not include either of the O'Donnell brothers. How could Albert have said such disgusting things about her? She only had one man, but she could tell by the look on Foster's face he believed her a whore. It hurt more than it should, much more. Foster had gotten into her heart and he had the ability to hurt her. She couldn't allow any man the power to hurt her again. She wished she knew what to do as soon as the storm stopped. There was a town close by. Maybe there would be a job for her there.

Tears trailed down her face again. How did she allow this to happen? It was all her fault. Looking at Molly, she didn't regret having her. She was just an innocent babe. She turned again and was surprised to see Foster sitting on a chair looking at her, petting Patches, who sat on his lap.

"I can't seem to get to sleep either, and I wanted to make sure you were all right." His brown eyes held so much compassion, her heart squeezed.

"I'm a survivor. You don't have to worry about me. I had hoped to never set eyes on him again."

"Yet you came here thinking it was his cabin."

"I had no other place to go. I prayed he wouldn't be here. He didn't seem the ranch type. I figured he had people running it for him. I just wanted somewhere to go until I got back on my feet. I don't think I'll be able to stay for Christmas after all. I need to get a job and support Molly and me."

He smiled. "Don't be in such a hurry. Heal and enjoy time with your daughter. Most jobs don't allow women to bring their children."

Her heart sank. "There must be something."

"Let's wait out the storm and then try to come up with something."

"You won't let Albert take me, will you?"

"No, you and Molly are under my protection. Truthfully I don't like the fact you came here knowing it was a horse ranch. I think you came to find Albert and part of you still loves him."

She drew in a short, quick breath. "I'm not sure how anyone could love him. I suppose I thought myself in love with him, but the minute he walked away, all kind feelings toward him shriveled, forever." She didn't like the anger she saw in his eyes. "I want you to know I never, well, he was the only one. His lies are appalling and hurtful. He and my father could have been made from the same cloth. While in Chicago, I was considered a poor relation, but I had a bit of respect. It was fleeting, but it was the only respect I ever felt. Until you. I used to see respect for the way I cared for Molly in your eyes. I'm sorry your feelings have turned to anger."

He glanced down at his folded hands and nodded. "I can't seem to help but feel duped. If you don't want to go with him, let me know." She started to answer and he held up his hand to stop her. "By rights he can take Molly with him. If you stay, I will take you to town as soon as it's safe so you can find your own way." He swallowed hard.

Nodding, she gave him a small smile. "Thank you for your kindness. I think I'll try to sleep again. Good night." She turned her back to him, but she could still feel the heat of his gaze on her. There would be no knight in shining armor, no prince to sweep her off her feet. She was on her own and the fact Albert could take Molly scared the hell out of her. She'd kill him before she'd allow him to do such a thing.

She must have slept deeply after she fed Molly again last night. She felt a pinch on her arm and her eyes blinked open. "Ouch." She gave Albert a hard stare. "What are you doing?"

"I'm going to save your pretty plump ass. All you have to do is call Foster inside, and I'll hit him hard over the head with this skillet."

"Excuse me? You want me to do what?"

"I want you to help kill him so we can have the ranch."

She sat up and checked on Molly. "Oh good Lord. You are out of your mind. Why do you want this ranch so much?"

"I just do. Now get up and do as I say, or Molly just might be accidentally dropped on her head. It could kill her, you know."

She got out of bed and wrapped a blanket around her. "No."

"What do you mean no?"

"You don't have a gun? What kind of man travels without a gun?"

"Foster took it."

"Very smart of him. Now get the idea of killing him out of your head." She walked over to the stove and poured herself some coffee.

"Why are you staring at me that way?" he whined.

129

"I'm trying to figure out what I ever saw in you. I don't see one attractive trait in you."

"I know why no one wanted you. You're an ugly old maid. You come from trash."

She put the coffee on the table and crossed her arms in front of her. "I don't care what you think. I'm not helping you."

The door opened wide. "Helping him do what?" Foster asked. Albert took an awkward swing at Foster with the heavy skillet and when Foster took a step back, Albert landed on the floor with the skillet still in his hand. Patches jumped on top of him and stared at him.

She laughed. "Well good, now I won't have to help you, dimwit." She poured another cup of coffee and handed it to Foster. "How bad is it out there? Are the horses all right?"

Albert shooed Patches away and sat up. "Like she really cares. She wouldn't know which end of the horse to feed."

"It's bad. We got more snow than I expected and the drifts have to be about twelve feet tall. The horses are all accounted for though." He took off his coat, stepped over Albert, and hung it up along with his hat on a wooden peg.

"That's the main thing," She said. "It's a good thing you tied the rope from the house to the barn."

"Funny thing. The rope had been cut."

Albert stood and adjusted his clothes. "Don't look at me. I bet it was miss innocent over there."

Foster gave him a pointed stare. "Give it up, Albert. I grew up with you and your no good ways. You wouldn't know the truth if it bit your ass. By the way, how did you get here?"

"A horse." Albert smirked.

"Damn you! Where is the horse?"

"I slapped his rump after I got here. I planned to stay for a while, plus you have plenty of horses."

"Are you just plain stupid or what? Never mind, I already know the answer." He grabbed his winter clothes off the peg and put them back on. "I'll be back."

"You're not going back out in the storm, are you?" she asked.

"I'll scout around for the horse. I have no idea if the horse is used to fending for itself or what. I have to look for it." He opened the door and glared at Albert. "You try anything at all and I'll put a bullet in you."

Albert's jaw dropped open. He started to say something but Foster was out the door before he got one word out.

"So, Albert what exactly is your plan? Kill Foster and take over the ranch? Those horses would scatter to the four winds if you tried to corral them. Some aren't even broke for riding. I know this may seem like an odd notion to you, but what about working? You know, get a job and earn your money."

"Shut your mouth before I shut it for you. You were looking for a rich husband, weren't you? It's the same thing. Foster got lucky with his horses. Why shouldn't he give his own brother at least half? It would be a whole lot safer for him if he saw things my way."

He must be daft. It was bad enough she was an inconvenience to Foster, but having Albert here was too much. "Why did you leave your horse out there?"

"It's not mine and I didn't want to unsaddle it." Molly began to cry. "Shut her up. That crying gets on my nerves."

Startled by his red mottled face, she quickly picked Molly up and rocked her. It took a bit of time but she finally settled down. What a sweet cherub. Ginger couldn't get enough of staring at her. She was a miracle. A real miracle.

"So, you had the baby here?"

"Yes, Foster helped."

"You let Foster see you like that? It's not decent." He frowned.

She laughed. "When you are in excruciating pain you don't care. There is nothing worth seeing, except for the baby."

"Show me your breasts." His voice grew husky.

"What are you saying? You are a disgusting pig." She held Molly to her shoulder.

"They seem much larger." He took a step toward her.

She hurried to the other side of the bed with Molly still asleep on her shoulder. She felt the wall against her back. "Stay away from me. You've done enough damage to my life, don't you think?"

"Like you say. I've already had you so having you again is no big deal."

"I can't even if I wanted to. I just had a baby. I'm healing from it." She shook her head and frowned. "You're welcome to go wander around in the snow if you like. Perhaps you'll get lost. I know you cut the rope. In case you didn't know it, we need Foster. He knows this land."

"Hell I got here and I can find my way out. As soon as the storm is over, you and the baby will come with me."

She cringed. "I don't think so."

"You'll do what I tell you."

FOSTER HEARD ARGUING from outside the house and stopped to listen. It was a sad thing for a man to have to eavesdrop on people in his own home. He shook his head. Damn Albert. Ginger was right, he was a pig. He stomped the snow off his boots before he opened the door. The frightened expression on Ginger's face as she clutched Molly to her was the last straw.

"I found your horse. I want you out of here come first light."

"But, but what about the snow?" Albert turned white.

"Then stay in the barn. You're not fit to be around people. You're not fit to be around livestock either, but this once I'll make an exception. Ginger is a guest in my house and she's to be treated with respect. I heard what you said to her, and you're way out of line. If there is any shame, it's yours for seducing an innocent for your supposed gain. You make me sick."

"I'll freeze," he whined.

"I could just put a bullet in your head and be done with you. No one would miss you. The horse might be missed but I'll bring it to town come spring. I doubt there will be questions." He walked over to the bed, held out his hand and his heart filled when she grabbed it. He helped her out of bed and held her close to his side. "It's almost Christmas and I for one don't plan to spend it fighting." He led Ginger to a chair and pulled it out for her to sit. "Have you eaten?"

Her blush was lovely. "Yes, thank you. What about you? Can I make you something?" A lump formed in his throat. No one had asked about his welfare since his mother died many years ago.

"I'm just fine. How's the little one fairing?" He cupped the back of Molly's head and stroked her fine hair.

"She's my daughter," Albert warned.

"She's lovely just like her mother," Foster continued, ignoring Albert. Ginger bestowed him with a bright smile. She filled his heart and no matter how many times he warned himself to not feel, it happened anyway. She'd be leaving come spring, but he couldn't help it.

He sat in a chair opposite her and stared at her. He would miss her so when she left, but for now he wanted to memorize her face for the long years to come.

"Like I said, she's my daughter. If I go to the barn so does she."

Ginger's eyes widened and she gasped. "You lost the right to be a father the minute you ran out on me. Molly belongs to me and only me! Stop trying to upset me. Molly doesn't feed as well when I'm upset."

Albert gazed intently at her chest. "We can't have that, can we?"

There was a knock on the door and Foster grabbed his shotgun. "Who is it?"

"Foster, let me in, my balls are freezing off."

He opened the door and laughed. "Damn, Younger, what the hell are you doing out in this weather? Come in and get warm."

Foster stepped aside and let his mountain of a friend in. He startled when Sheriff Younger pulled his gun. "Get up!" he growled as he motioned toward Albert.

"Albert, this here is Sheriff Younger. I'd do what he says. He's known for his shoot now and ask questions later way of doing things." Patches walked in a circle between the sheriff's legs, brushing up against him.

Ginger started to stand and Foster guided her back to the bed. "Stay put."

"What's he wanted for, Younger?"

"Murder. Mind tying him up for me? I could use a cup of coffee. You know I didn't see the storm coming."

"Who'd he kill?"

"Sam at the livery stable. I have three witnesses. And he stole a horse."

"How's Sam's family?"

"Tessa and the little ones will be in a bind this winter. The town is helping all they can. Bringing in this piece of sh- er- dirt will help."

Foster grabbed a rope and tied Albert to the chair. "I

knew you were no good, but murder? I hope they hang you."
He shook his head in disgust. "Why didn't you just pay for
the horse?"

"I didn't have any money. He was in my way."

Younger poured himself some coffee and nodded at
Ginger. "Ma'am." He sat down and smiled. "You old dog, I
didn't know you had a wife and baby. Congratulations."

"The bitch had my baby!" Albert raged.

Foster shook his head. Here was the opportunity to turn
things to rights. He could save Ginger's reputation and undo
all the evil Albert had heaped on her. He had the chance to
make Molly's birth legitimate and he was taking it. "This is
my wife, Ginger and my daughter Molly. Albert here is my
stepbrother. Tried to kill me with a skillet."

"Nice to meet you, Ginger. I'm so glad my friend here
finally found himself a good woman."

Albert snorted.

"A skillet you say?" Sheriff Younger laughed. "What
happened to his gun?"

"I took it from him. He would have used it if he had it. He
wanted my ranch and my wife."

"Some are pure evil. Mind if I fill my belly before
we go?"

Ginger stood and lay Molly down in her crate. "Surely
you won't go back out into the storm."

"Wish I could stay a spell, but my Laura is expecting me
back for Christmas and I promised. She'd love to meet you.
She's always going on how Foster needs a wife. I'll be happy
to report not only does he have a beautiful, sweet wife but he
has a daughter as well."

"Will you be home by then?" she asked.

"If I can borrow a horse."

"I can do one better. I found the horse he stole wandering
around. Take it back to Tessa and tell her I'll be in town as

soon as possible to help her out with the horses. Sorry you had to come all the way out here."

Younger wiped his mouth with his sleeve. "It's my job." He stood and untied Albert from the chair and retied his hands in front of him. "Come on, you murdering horse thief. Now I just want to make one thing clear. Dead or alive, I don't really care that's up to you. Got it?"

Albert nodded as he glared at Ginger. "You know damn well you and that baby are mine." She shrunk back as the sheriff dragged Albert from the house.

"I'll be right back. I want to saddle the horse and get them on their way. Are you alright?"

She gave him a small smile and nodded.

GINGER SAT on the bed in shock. Albert murdered a man? Oh good Lord, he'd been serious about getting rid of Foster the whole time. Her stomach churned and a shiver ran down her spine. She'd brought danger to Foster. He'd made the ultimate sacrifice by claiming her as his wife but he didn't mean it. She'd be gone before his first trip to town. He could tell people she died or something. She'd just have to go in another direction. Montana was full of towns.

She'd never known anyone as kind as Foster, and she'd never find another like him. Imagine, the sheriff's wife thought Foster needed a wife. He didn't want one or he'd have one already. He liked his quiet solitude and she'd invaded it tenfold. More than tenfold and the best way to thank him was to leave him be.

Her heart squeezed. He'd become more than a stranger to her the last few days. She'd learned one thing in life; you can't always have what you want. Life was full of difficulties and sometimes just being safe from beatings and awful men was enough. Love would have been nice but with Molly in the picture, her hopes dimmed. She could claim to be a widow but more lies just didn't set well with her.

The howling of the wind outside reminded her she had time to come up with a plan. Foster would know about the towns nearby. He might even take her to one of them. She smiled. Imagine that big bear of a sheriff had a wife. She'd never seen anyone as big. Albert wouldn't have a chance to escape his fate this time. She didn't feel bad for him at all.

Molly began to cry and Ginger untied the front of her dress and fed her. The cold came in with Foster and he glanced at her but quickly looked away. She smiled.

"They are on their way. I knew he was a bad seed but murder? I figured him too inept to do it. I'm sorry you ever got involved with him."

"Me too. I led him to your door and I apologize." She sighed.

"He would have come anyway. He was broke. I think he planned to winter here then steal the horses. How, I have no idea, the damn fool can hardly sit a horse. He's gone and hopefully it's forever." He put more wood on the fire.

"Thank you for trying to defend my honor. You didn't have to lie about me being your wife. There will be questions once I'm gone."

"Is that what you want to do? Leave come spring?"

"Of course."

He poured himself some coffee, sat down and stared at it. He looked to be deep in thought. He probably regretted claiming her. It was said on impulse and by now Albert had probably convinced the sheriff the truth about her. It hurt knowing she would just bring embarrassment to Foster.

She finished burping Molly and put her back down to sleep. Getting up, she went to the door and opened it. The winter storm was raging, blowing one direction then

137

another. The cold went right to her bones and she instantly had snow in her hair and eyelashes. What an amazing sight. Warmth came behind her and she felt Foster's strong arm snake around her middle and haul her back against him.

"What are you doing?" His warm breath blew into her ear.

"Just looking. It's been storming inside and out today." He gently led her inside and closed the door.

"It sure has, but now the storm inside is over." He turned her until she faced him and encircled her with his arms. "Your life hasn't been easy." His big brown eyes were so full of concern, tears trailed down her face.

"I'm sorry. I'm not much of a crier, but lately I'm a watering pot. I have so many emotions running through me."

"Here, let's sit and you can tell me." He pulled two chairs in front of the fire. He waited until she sat before he did. Putting both elbows on his knees, he leaned forward. "You know you're safe here, don't you?"

She dashed her tears with the backs of her hands and nodded. "I do thank you for that. I owe you so much I can never repay."

"Who's asking for repayment? I happen to like your company." He smiled.

"It's nice of you to say, but I can tell you enjoy living alone with the cat. I'm, we're an intrusion. It's my own fault I allowed Albert to touch me. I could have said no. My decision hurt so many people, including Molly. I mean, I'll do my best by her. What that will be I don't know yet, but I will keep her safe no matter what. I put you in danger, I mortified my aunt, and I enraged my father. I'm disappointed in myself, yet I feel proud all at the same time. It makes no sense."

"Actually it does." He took her hand in his large one and gave it a squeeze. "We've all done things we regret and sometimes it leads us down a different path than we imagined and yes people can get hurt along the way but that wasn't your intent. Don't forget you had help. Albert preys on people for money. Did he ask your aunt for money to stay quiet?"

Startled she nodded. "How?"

"It's his way of life. He'd rather play games with other people's lives than make an honest dollar. I'm sure your aunt could have quietly found you a husband if she paid Albert off. I've lived alone by choice, mostly due to Albert and his father. I know there are good people in the world, but I can't stop wondering if I'll end up treating a wife and child the same way they treated my mother and me. I'm a grown man and I know better, but something always holds me back from loving someone."

Disappointment flowed through her. Everything he said was understandable, including the part where he wouldn't give his heart to another. Damn her romantic heart and dreams. "Thank you for trying to assuage my guilt. I've been blaming myself so long; I didn't look at it any other way."

"I admire you. I don't know anyone who'd walk miles to give birth to a baby. You have gumption." His voice lowered as he gazed into her eyes.

She quickly glanced away. No more pretend dreams. "Molly seems to be thriving and for that I'm grateful."

"She is a little doll. You're a good mother to her."

"I'm trying and will always try to do right by her. She's all I have left. We'll have a good life, I expect." She still couldn't look at him with her eyes full of doubt.

"I need to take care of some things out in the barn. Get some rest. You were up with Molly plenty last night." He gave her hand another quick squeeze before he stood and put on his coat and hat. She gave him a quick smile before he left.

He was right, she needed to rest.

CHAPTER FOUR

*C*hristmas was tomorrow and here he was hiding out in the barn. He'd shot a buck earlier and they would have fresh venison for their feast. Ginger sure knew how to cook. He'd never had better. He never had cause to celebrate Christmas before and he wasn't sure what else was needed. There wasn't time for presents. He smiled. He'd never really wanted to give anyone a present before. He had one thing of value but it wasn't appropriate to give to Ginger.

She wouldn't want it anyway. She was so determined to leave him. She never mentioned him claiming her as his wife and Molly as his child. What had he expected? A declaration of love? A happy ending? He knew better. He wasn't sure how it happened, but he couldn't let her leave, not without telling her how he felt. The lilt of her voice, the way she cocked her head to one side, exposing her beautiful neck, her care of Molly, the list could go on forever.

Damn it was cold, but he needed to cool off. Last night he lay on the floor with Patches watching her each time she fed Molly and to his horror, it aroused him to see her full breasts. What he wouldn't have given to be able to just touch them. He could hardly look at her this morning for fear she'd see his desire in his eyes. He didn't want her disgust. The curves of her body did things to him he couldn't explain. Things he didn't want.

He decided long ago to forego love and family for sanity. The volatile relationship his mother had with his stepfather turned him sour on marriage. Any time he'd tried to get close to a woman he always ended up sorry he even tried. However, Ginger made his heart pound painfully against his chest, she took up all his thoughts, and she made his pants feel too small. He shook his head. He knew better than to act like a randy cowboy.

He was no good for her anyway. She needed someone who knew how to love. Someone who knew how to be gentle and giving. He wasn't sure he knew how to do any of it. He was often away from the house for days at a time when he was rounding up horses. No, he wasn't husband material. Somehow, he'd have to keep his eyes off her. As if it would be possible.

He left the barn and a gust of wind almost toppled him. He prayed Younger made it back to town unharmed. As for Albert, he could just go to hell. He grabbed more wood from the front of the house and opened the door. The wind took it and it banged hard against the house. Before he could drop the logs, Ginger was there trying to wrestle the door closed.

"Leave it, you shouldn't be exerting yourself. I have to go back out anyway." His voice was gruffer than he would have liked, and he noticed a sense of sadness as he passed by her. Damn women could be so sensitive. He made three more trips and finally took off his coat. "I think we have enough wood. You never know. Montana winters can be bad. I've been snowed in before." She shivered. "We'll get through. No worries."

"I have complete confidence in you, Foster. You are a

capable man and I'm lucky I ended up at your ranch. It seems naive now that I'd even find the cabin but I had no choice. I do believe to have been blessed."

His heart fluttered at her smile. He had to look away. He crossed the room and began to stack the wood neatly. The cabin had always seemed adequate to him, but now it was too small. There was a lack of breathing room. How the heck was he supposed to be a gentleman and not think wicked thoughts about her? Was it wicked if he really cared for her? At least he had something else to think about instead of her luscious breasts.

"Foster?"

He turned to her. "What?"

"I was asking if you had any Christmas memories you'd like to share with me." Her lips tempted him.

"It was just another day of chores. I knew it was Christmas because of the decorations in town and the other kids talked about the pennies and oranges that were left in their stockings by Santa Claus."

"Same here. It was a day to drink extra so any money we might have had for a meal went for whiskey. One time we had a neighbor who took pity on me. She came to get me one year. I had a fine time. There were platters of food and sweets. I'd never seen the like. Under the tree lay stacks of presents, and they gave me one. Mrs. Bunting made a new scarf. I remember my happiness when I wrapped the red scarf around my neck." Her smile dimmed. "My father came looking for me and made a scene. He grabbed the scarf from my neck, threw it to the ground and stomped on it all while Mrs. Bunting and her family watched." She gazed at Molly. "I don't even know why I asked. It just brought up bad memories." She shrugged her shoulders.

"The good thing about life is you sometimes get a second

chance. A chance to make new memories. What do you say we sing a couple of those Christmas songs?"

"What a lovely idea, Foster," she gushed, her eyes glowing.

They sang song after song until they could think of no more. He couldn't remember a better time. He'd thought her attractive before, but nothing compared to her beauty when she was happy.

"You're staring at me. Is something wrong?" she asked, her voice full of worry.

He shook his head. "No, in fact I was just admiring you. You're beautiful."

She pressed her palms to her reddened cheeks. "You need better eyes, Foster. I suppose my plainness made it easier for Albert to turn my head. All he had to do was pay attention to me." Her body sagged.

"It's not true, you know. You are far from plain. Both you and Molly are very pretty. I have no idea why anyone would think otherwise. You've been handed some bad blows but here you are, safe with a new daughter. You're a fierce one."

Ginger shook her head. "You somehow give me the confidence to feel fierce. Oh, Molly needs to be fed. She sure has a healthy cry." She got up and began undoing the front of her dress before she even got to the bed. The lamplight made her red hair radiate with highlights of all colors of red and a bit of blonde. She sat and cooed to Molly and he looked away.

She stirred him like no other but they really didn't know each other. He put his hand in his pants pocket and fingered the thin gold band he'd put in there. It would be so easy to ask her to marry him, yet it was plain crazy. He'd be tied to her forever and what if he changed his mind? Worse, what if she changed her mind? She was in a bind and she might accept his proposal to have a roof over her head. His chest tightened.

She'd be there until spring. Perhaps there was no hurry.

He just wanted to give her something for Christmas. He didn't deal well with feelings, and being alone was a sight better than being undecided. No more telling her she was pretty. He didn't need the hassle of a wife and child. There, it was all figured out. Why did he feel so lost?

"It's getting late," she whispered from the bed. "I'm going to go to sleep once Molly is done here."

"Fine. Good night." He grabbed a few furs and blankets and put them on the floor. He stripped off his shirt and took off his boots, his spine tingling the whole time. Glancing toward the bed, he realized she watched him. Damn, now his pants were too tight again. He laid down with his back to her and closed his eyes, listening to her sing to Molly. Did his mother ever sing to him? Maybe once upon a time, but once she married his stepfather the singing stopped. He heard the rustling of her taking off her dress and he made himself concentrate on his breathing. In and out, in and out.

GINGER WOKE to silence and immediately looked for Molly. It had been a sleepless night. Molly cried incessantly and nothing helped. In the wee hours of the morning, she finally settled down.

"Shhh," Foster whispered. He sat near the stove with Molly in his arms and she slept. It was a breathless sight to see such a big strong man cuddle a tiny baby. If she didn't already care for him, this moment would have done it. Her heart felt near to bursting.

Maybe she'd been led to this place for a reason. Maybe she and Foster were meant to be together. He thought her pretty, he enjoyed her company, and he was sweet with Molly.

"How long have you been holding her?" She smiled.

"Almost two hours now. I wanted you to get some sleep."

"Oh my, that's a long time. Thank you. I think she knows she's safe in your arms." Their gazes met and held for a moment before Foster frowned and looked away.

"If you're up to taking her, I have a path to make through the snow to the barn and hopefully one to check on the horses." He handed her the baby with minimal touching and put on his coat and hat. He walked out of the cabin without another word.

She stared at the door, disappointed. She'd read him wrong last night. Once again, she took something as simple as friendship and romanticized it. When was she ever going to learn? It made her sick to her stomach. He didn't think of her that way. She didn't blame him. She tried to remind herself he liked to be alone but somewhere along the line hope budded and her imagination followed.

"Merry Christmas, Molly." She kissed the baby's forehead and set her on the bed. Quickly she put on her dress and began to make breakfast. She'd earn her keep, and it would feel less like a friendship and more like an employee relationship. Tears burned as she swallowed the huge lump in her throat. Happy endings were for other girls, not for her. Perhaps if she was more educated, or prettier, or whatever Foster liked... She sighed as her heart dropped. Somehow, she managed to make breakfast and have everything ready for when Foster returned.

He came in looking chilled to the bone. She quickly helped him off with his coat and hung it up for him. "Thanks." He continued to the table and sat down. "Looks good."

She poured them both coffee and sat at her place, across from him. "Merry Christmas."

He nodded. "Merry Christmas. Thank you such a fine meal."

"It's the least I can do to earn my keep." She watched him nod and sadness whirled around her. She'd never grow up and be realistic. Her stupid heart wouldn't let her, it just ached. Why did everything have to be so hard?

"Tell me more about your ranch."

"Why?" His question stunned her.

"No reason. Just making conversation." Her face heated and her appetite fled.

"I'm surprised Albert didn't tell you all about it. He planned a big payday and he asked you to join him," he said, his voice laced with bitterness.

"I don't like the direction this conversation is going. You saw how Albert treated me. Did you see a couple in love? A couple who wanted to be together? Have I once asked you for money? I admit I knew about this place, but even though you don't like me, I'm glad I came for Molly's sake. She's alive because of you. She wasn't thrown out in the freezing snow to die. I know I'll never have much to give her but I gave her a chance at life." The wind began to howl. "I wish that incessant wind would just stop. As soon as it stops we'll be leaving." Taking a deep breath, she let it out slowly as she willed herself not to cry. Despite her efforts, tears started to flow and she got up and went to the bed, pretending to check on Molly. Her shoulders shook and she didn't fool him. He had to know she was crying.

She'd been a complete fool and now she was crying. She couldn't summon up an ounce of dignity. It all became too much. Albert taking advantage of her, being sent home in disgrace, her father's abuse, threats, and now Foster thought her capable of stealing his land.

"I'll be back." The door opened and closed.

Now she needed to get ahold of herself. Taking some warm water, she washed her face and brushed her hair. Thankfully, Molly still slept. It didn't matter if her heart was broken; they were stuck with each other for a long while. The cabin was too small to harbor bad feelings.

She made quick work of the dishes, cut up venison, potatoes, and carrots and put them on the stove to cook. She also put together a peach cobbler. Thank goodness for jarred fruit. It took a while but she finally calmed, fed Molly and sat petting Patches, waiting for Foster to come back. It was his home and he should be able to be in it without a weepy woman in it.

———

THE HORSES WERE fine but he stood out in the freezing wind watching them. Why had he treated Ginger like that? Damn his big mouth. He knew she had nothing to do with the plan to take his ranch. He was just grasping at any excuse not to like her. Somehow, while he held Molly last night he knew he loved them both. He pictured himself teaching a young Molly to ride a horse. He also pictured Ginger in bed with him. He wanted her in his life, not only his bed.

How was he supposed to go back into the house after making her cry? Should he apologize or act as if it never happened? He'd rarely seen men and women interact with each other. Not in a good way. How did one apologize to a woman? A plain sorry wasn't going to cut it and there were no flowers to be found. Damn, double damn. It was too cold to stay outside. It took more courage to walk back into the house than facing down a bear.

He opened the door and peered in. Ginger was stirring something that smelled great, and Molly slept. He hoped Ginger would turn around, but she didn't. Straightening his shoulders he made his way to her. He stood right behind her. "Ginger?"

She turned and gave him a wobbly smile. "You're back."

"I am. I'm no good with people. I'm good with horses but not people. I wanted to bring flowers to say I'm sorry but all I have is this." He took his hand from behind his back and opened it.

"A snowball?" Her lips twitched.

"A snowball. You can throw it at my face if you like." He waited anxiously for her reaction.

She took it into her hands and stared at it. "You know, this is the most thoughtful gift I've ever gotten. I'm tempted to throw it at you, but I want harmony in this house. I don't want my actions to drive you away." She walked around him, opened the door, and carefully placed it on the ground. "There. If I need it I know where it is." Closing the door, she turned toward him. "I'm sorry my crying made you uncomfortable. I'll try to be more cheerful."

"Just be yourself. I'm not sure why I said those things to you. I'm sorry." He held his breath.

"Me too," she said and he slowly let his breath out as a huge weight lifted off his shoulders.

"Something smells good."

"Venison stew and a surprise." Her smile lit up the whole cabin. He could see the peach dessert on the counter, but made no mention of it. He'd be surprised for her sake.

There was silence, and it became awkward. Had they run out of things to say so soon? "Spring won't be coming anytime soon. It was predicted to be a bad winter."

"I heard people talk about how bad it was supposed to be, and they were right. I shudder when I think about what could have happened to me out there. Molly and I would be dead for sure."

"You'd have found somewhere to go for safety. You're very strong and brave."

"I'm not sure if it was bravery or stupidity that made me leave my home."

"It was the love of a mother, and that can be a powerful thing. My mother loved me but could only express it with her eyes. I could see how proud she was of me, but she never dared to say it." His heart warmed at the memory.

"What happened to Albert's mother?"

"I only know she died. They never talked about her and I knew better than to ask." He sat down at the table, leaning his elbows on it.

"I slept on the ground for a long time. I built the barn when I had time, but I knew I had to have it done before winter. It wasn't easy, but I did it. The following year I built the house while building my herd." He sat down at the table, leaning his elbows on it. "I understand horses better than people. That's why I find them, and break them to saddle. I've raised quite a few, and it's been a labor of love. Don't get me wrong, there are plenty of long days and sleepless nights, but I feel as though I belong here. I left home right after my mother died. I was fourteen, and there was no reason to stay. I worked on a few ranches and saved every penny I made. I'd had my eye on this piece of land for a long time, and the day I bought it I was so very proud of my accomplishment."

"You should be proud."

"I've eked out a living but recently landed a contract with the Army. I have a feeling Albert heard about it and decided to take what was mine."

Ginger poured coffee for them both and handed a cup to him. "He did say it was prosperous." She sat across from him and her face paled. "I still can't fathom I believed him and he's Molly's father. What am I going to tell her?"

He wished she could tell Molly he was her father. He wouldn't have minded if what he told the sheriff was true and they were both his. She was unlike anyone he'd ever met, and she made his blood fill with excitement. She and Molly had cast the loneliness of winter away.

"Well, I guess I'll figure something out. Who knows, I might even find a husband before she's old enough to know the difference." She sipped her coffee and adeptly avoided his gaze. "I need to bake the surprise." She rose and turned away from him. He enjoyed the view.

He fingered the ring in his pocket and decided it wasn't fitting. She wouldn't want a ring from him. It was just as well, but his heart didn't agree. Molly began to fuss and he quickly went to the bed. "I'll change her." He grabbed a clean cloth and began to change her. He felt the heat of Ginger's gaze and glanced up. "What?" She had the most incredulous expression on her face.

"Never in my life have I heard of a man changing a diaper. You do it with such ease. You're a good man, Foster."

His face grew warm. He wrapped Molly in a blanket and carried her to the table, where he sat holding her in his arms. He already thought of her as his own. He just needed to convince her mama. "She's lovely. Just like her mother."

Ginger stood in the middle of the cabin with her eyes widened and her jaw dropped. "She is pretty but—"

"Don't even try to object. I think you're beautiful and that's that." The wide smile she bestowed him filled him with pleasure. Molly stared at him and cooed. He put his finger in her hand and she gripped it. "A strong one, aren't you?"

"She sure is, isn't she? You'd best hand her over so I can feed her." She held out her arms.

"She's not crying yet. Maybe she likes being in my arms."

"Any girl would... I mean."

He laughed and flashed a grin at her. Maybe he could earn her trust before spring after all. A sense of peace engulfed him. Yes, maybe he could. Just then, Molly let out an ear-splitting cry, and he handed her over. The wind kicked up and something began to bang. "Sounds like the barn door. I'd better have a look."

She sat on the bed with Molly and nodded. "Be careful."
His heart squeezed. It'd been awhile since anyone cared.

SHE WATCHED him leave and wondered if she glowed on the
outside as much as the inside. He'd made her feel special. It
was so different from the way Albert made her feel. Foster
talked from his heart. Sometimes when he looked at her, her
body tingled. It was a very strange feeling. He also told her
his plans for his ranch and how he struggled to make it prosperous. Could it be he trusted her? Men were so contrary.
She never understood them, but she did know Foster was a
kind, gentle man. He didn't seem the type to try to say pretty
things to her for gain. He had nothing to gain.

He had nothing to gain. She breathed in and out slowly,
thinking the words over. He actually liked her? He obviously
had taken to Molly. There was something different about
him. It was almost as if he decided to let his guard down. His
lot in life hadn't been easy and not trusting came with the
territory. She well knew it. A seed planted began to bloom
and she gave thanks. She was on the cusp of happiness, but it
still scared her. She doubted her ability to be a good judge of
character. Everything in her being screamed to give him a
chance but something held her back.

How she wanted to take the leap, take the chance, but
truthfully, he hadn't made a declaration of love. Maybe she
was reading into things and there was no way she'd allow
herself to be crushed by a man again. Molly fell asleep before
finishing her feeding. Being a mother was joyous enough. It
was the best Christmas present she'd ever had.

The wind howled louder and louder, and she swore the
house shook. She opened the door looking for Foster, but the
world was a mass of whiteness. The snow whipped and

whirled across the plains. There was no way to see the barn, and she hoped Foster was safe. Thank goodness he'd tied another rope from the house to the barn. Could the horses survive in this weather? It took all her strength to fight the door closed.

She removed the cobbler from the stove and stirred the stew. She'd found a needle and thread the day before. Grabbing them and a ripped shirt of Foster's, she sat at the table mending it. As it grew late, she worried. She lit the lantern and turned it up higher than needed in case Foster needed a beacon to follow. Something wasn't right, she felt it deep down.

She got up from the table and checked on Molly. Then she put on her coat and hat and grabbed the lantern before stepping out into the storm. Thank goodness for the rope. She'd taken only a few steps from the house and already she had the feeling of being turned all around. She could barely see a step before her. A few times she fell and struggled to get up. It was nearly impossible to keep ahold of both the rope and lantern. The wind tried its best to push her back, but finally she made it to the barn. The door was still open and banging. She hadn't heard it over the sound of the wind.

She stumbled into the barn and held the lantern high. At first, she didn't see Foster until she walked toward one of the stalls. There he was on the ground with an apple-sized lump on his forehead. Damn, a horse had kicked him. She hesitated and looked for the horse before going into the stall, but there was no sign of the horse. It probably rode out into the storm.

"Foster, can you hear me?" she asked as she fell to her knees next to him. Running her hand over the rest of his head, she found no other injury. "Foster?"

He groaned loudly before he let out a string of curse words. "The horse?"

"Gone. We need to get you back to the house. It was so hard to get here but going back the wind will be behind us. It might make it easier." She stared into his dazed eyes, hoping his injury was superficial. "Let's get you sitting up first." She got behind him and pulled him until he was leaning against the stall wall. He was heavier than she thought. She'd never had to drag anyone but her father before, and he wasn't a big man at all.

"Please, God," she whispered.

"Where's Molly?" he asked his voice husky.

"She's home, we need to get back."

"Home, that sounds nice." He helped to push himself up to a standing position. "Whoa. I'm dizzy. Give me a minute." He closed his eyes. "Okay, let's do this. We need to get to Molly."

She led the way, making sure he was behind her with each step. Her face burned in the cold and her fingers were beginning to numb, but she held on to the rope for all she was worth. They only fell twice, and it was hard getting them both up, but they pushed onward until they bumped into the cabin door. Ginger opened the door and they both landed on the floor. She quickly got back up and fought the wind to close the door.

Molly was still asleep and Ginger wanted to cry in relief. "Here let's get those wet clothes off you," she said as she helped him to stand. "Come; sit in front of the stove." She quickly took off her coat and hat and with fingers that hurt unbearably, she began to undress Foster. Luckily, he had gloves on and his hands looked fine. After she got his coat, hat, gloves, and boots off he still shivered uncontrollably. She needed to warm him through or he'd die.

It was no time to be shy or worry about what was right. She needed to strip them both down and get into bed. Foster didn't object as she removed his clothes. He didn't say much of anything as she laid him on the bed. Next, she took off her clothes and climbed into bed.

She was much warmer than Foster, and it felt as though he was stealing her heat, but she lay on top of him, willing to give it to him. He shivered through the night and cried out when she had to leave his body to feed Molly. He sighed in relief when she returned. The fact he was still cold worried her, as did his head wound. She did all she knew and tried to keep him warm. It was hard not to notice how muscular he was. He had a sprinkling of chest hair and his shoulders were much broader than hers were. Perhaps she didn't have enough heat for such a large man.

Even with all the worry, she had butterflies in her stomach from being so close to this man. He'd saved her and she was glad to try to return the favor.

———

SOMETHING WAS ON HIS CHEST. He opened his eyes and was pleasantly surprised to find Ginger on top of him. Usually it was the cat on his chest. He lay perfectly still and enjoyed the feel of her body against his. What happened? How could he have taken Ginger and not known? His head hurt and he remembered. Slowly he wrapped his arms around her and tucked her head under his chin. It felt so good to cradle her against him. Not only physically but his heart sang. She must have gotten him out of the barn. He closed his eyes again. Yes, he remembered her leading him to the house and undressing him.

Damn it must have cost her dignity a lot to get naked and crawl on top of him. Would most women have done it? Somehow he had a feeling some would have considered it too improper. He was lucky indeed.

She stirred and snuggled deeper against him. He kissed

the top of her head and stroked her back as he looked over at Molly. He was surprised to see her blue eyes looking back at him. Usually she was either sleeping or feeding. She waved her little fists in the air, seeming content to watch him. He wanted this this so badly. He wanted them to be a family. To have Ginger's love would be the greatest gift.

"How long have you been awake?" she asked sleepily.

"A few minutes. I've been watching Molly stare at me." Ginger started to move, but he tightened his arms around her. "Thank you for what you did. You saved my life and you didn't have to. You never think of yourself and I admire you."

She raised her head up and stared at him with awe in her eyes. "You're the one to be admired. I think very highly of you."

He stroked the nape of her neck. "Do you now?"

"Yes I do."

He dragged her up toward his face to kiss her and groaned as she slid across his most sensitive area. He grew hard, and he saw the fright in her eyes. "Hey, I would never. Besides, you just had a baby, and you need to heal. I can't help my reaction to you, but I don't have to do anything about it. I like having you in my arms." He lifted his head and pressed his lips against her soft, plump ones. It was a kiss worth waiting for. Her response surprised him as she kissed him back in ardor. When she opened her mouth for him, he slid his tongue inside. She tasted of sweetness and he didn't want the kiss to end. It felt so right to be with her, so natural. He needed another taste, but Molly cried out.

Ginger ended the kiss but gave him a loving smile before she gently got off him. "I think you're nice and warm now."

He laughed. "More than warm. You're one hell of a woman." He loved how her whole body blushed as she reached for a blanket to cover her.

"I'll get up and give you some privacy." He sat up and groaned.

"Your head?"

"It was quite a kick. Unexpected too." He lay back down.

"Stay in bed. I'm sure you shouldn't be out of bed with a head injury. Just close your eyes."

Although tempted, he couldn't close his eyes and miss her dressing. She glanced at him a few times and frowned. He frowned back. One minute she kissed him back for all she was worth and the next she threw frowns his way. There was no figuring women out, but damn, he really wished he could figure her out. He watched as she changed and fed Molly. He smiled as Patches tried to climb onto Ginger's lap.

"Thank you for saving me, by the way," he said, hoping to start a conversation.

"No thanks needed." She finally set Molly down and then added a few logs to the fire. She was quite proficient in the kitchen, he observed, as she made coffee and pancakes.

"Well, thank you anyway. I could have frozen to death if you hadn't helped me back and gotten into bed with me."

Her whole face grew a fiery red. "Listen, just because I did what was necessary doesn't mean I'll jump into bed with you again." She put her hands on her hips and gave him a sour look.

"I didn't mean it that way, so you can stop making faces at me."

"Making faces? Really? I hadn't realized," she said, her voice heavy with sarcasm.

"Why exactly are you mad at me?"

She shook her head. "I'm not mad at you." She sighed. "I'm mad at myself for enjoying your arms around me."

He gave her his best grin. "Did you enjoy the kiss too?" He cocked his left brow.

"No." She turned away from him and continued cooking.

What did she mean no? Who wouldn't have found pleasure in that kiss? She moaned, didn't she? Maybe she didn't. Was he a bad kisser? He hadn't had very much practice. Damn now, he didn't know what to think.

"We never did have that peach cobbler you made."

"We'll have it tonight." She didn't turn around.

He shook his head. She must have enjoyed Albert's kisses better. "How many men have you kissed?"

She turned and her eyes narrowed. "How many do think I've kissed?"

"I don't know. I was wondering whose kisses you liked. You must be comparing me to someone."

She took the pancakes off the stove and stood at the foot of the bed tapping her foot. "For your information I have kissed two men, Albert and you. There is no comparison."

His heart dropped. "He's that good of a kisser?"

"No he is not. He slobbers and I couldn't wait to get away."

"So, you didn't like his or mine?"

"For the love of God, what is the matter with you? You have no real interest in me, so stop. Just stop talking about kisses. Breakfast will be ready in a minute." Shaking her head, she turned away and stalked to the stove.

No real interest? He thought she was a bit sweet on him. He was doubly glad he didn't give her the ring for Christmas. His heart started to ice over, and he had the urge to hit something. He never should have allowed her into his heart. He glanced over at Molly, and his heart started to warm again. It was going to be one hell of a long winter, being with someone who didn't like you. He sat up and gingerly touched the bump on his head.

"Do you think it's as big as it feels?"

She stiffened and slowly turned around. "Oh I could feel it, but I didn't look. Why would you ask me a question like that? It's no wonder you're not married." She quickly went back to cooking.

"Ginger?"

"I don't want to talk to you."

"What did you think I meant?"

"You are a pest this morning. I know what you meant. I didn't look at yours, and I didn't look at Albert's either. However, if you really have to know yours is much bigger. There, are you happy now? Maybe we shouldn't talk until spring." She huffed and promptly ignored him.

His lips twitched. She thought he was asking about his privates. He bit the inside of his cheek to stop the roar of laughter begging to escape. He didn't know why, but he puffed up with pride knowing his was bigger. No not bigger, much bigger. Finally, he couldn't contain his laughter. It rumbled from deep within, and once he started he couldn't seem to stop. She frowned at him, gaped at him, threatened to kill him, but he still laughed. When she asked what was so funny, he only laughed harder.

Molly started to cry, and Ginger quickly picked her up. She gave him a murderous look before she tried to calm the baby.

He finally stopped laughing and stared at them longingly. He wasn't making any headway with her at all. In fact, things seemed worse. "I'm sorry. Why don't you bring her here?"

She hesitated then walked to the side of the bed. "I don't like being laughed at." The hurt in her eyes saddened him. She handed him Molly and walked away.

"I hurt you. I care for you too much to want to hurt you." Silence ensued and he could have kicked himself for revealing his feelings.

She stared at him. "I lied when I said I didn't like your kisses. I'm embarrassed I'm the type of woman who takes her clothes off and jumps in bed with you. I bet most ladies

159

would have balked at the very notion. I can't help but think you must have a low opinion of me. I had Molly out of wedlock and I shamed myself by sleeping with you." A lone tear trailed down her face. "Growing up everyone whispered I would end up to be no good like my father, and they were right. It doesn't matter where I go, I always do something wrong. I plan to change that when Molly and I leave, God willing."

"God willing you will leave or God willing you plan to change?" He held his breath.

"Both perhaps. I don't know. I know the best way to repay your kindness is to get out of your life. You don't want to be saddled with me. You may think you care for me but you just feel sorry for me."

"Is that what you really think? I feel sorry for you? I wish I could leap out of this bed and show you how sorry I don't feel. I care for you more than I've ever cared before. You can't change the way I feel and you did nothing shameful, nothing. You saved my life by giving me your heat. If you hadn't climbed in with me, we wouldn't be having this discussion. You gave me a wonderful Christmas present. I'm greedy though. I want the greatest gift."

"The greatest gift?" Her brow furrowed.

"You'll figure it out, and it has nothing to do with your body." He wanted to smile at her but he didn't want her to cry again. "Tell you what. I'll trade you Molly for some pancakes."

She gave him a half smile. "My pancakes are that good, are they?"

"You are an exceptional cook." He watched in pleasure as she blushed and smiled deeply. She went back to the stove, piled some pancakes on a plate, and traded them for Molly.

"I got the better end of the deal," she said.

"I don't know, sweetheart. I think she needs changing."

He certainly was a mystery. He was right about one thing; she shouldn't feel shame for saving him last night. He called it a gift and perhaps it was. She did it without thinking about anything else but saving him. What was the greatest gift he talked about? The only great gift she could think of she already gave to Albert. She's been told from an early age her virginity was the greatest gift but Foster thought something else was. Her eyes widened.

"I won't give you such a gift."

His mouth dropped open. "What?"

"Molly is my daughter and she stays with me."

"Of course she does, honey. I didn't mean to upset you." He handed her his empty plate. "I'm going to get out of bed."

"I think you should rest. That bump on your head looks big…" She swallowed hard. "Is that what you meant? The bump on your head? You knew I misunderstood and laughed about it?"

His lips twitched and he started laughing again.

"Stop laughing."

He laughed louder. "I can't."

"The reason yours is much bigger is because Albert doesn't have a bump on his head." She gave him a curt nod expecting the laughter to stop, but it only started it up again. Staring him down didn't help either. She approached him, ready to swat him when he grabbed her around the waist and pulled her down onto the bed. She sputtered and tried to get up, but he held her tight.

"Listen, I want our life to be one of love and laughter. I want to share the sun and the stars with you. I want us to build the finest ranch around. I want to be your husband and Molly's father. I want the greatest gift; your love."

Lying on her back, she stared at him in surprise. "You love

me? My love is the greatest gift?" She gave him a smile of love. "I thought you didn't want a wife."

"I didn't, but somehow you changed all that. I've never known anyone so selfless and kind. You are loving and strong. I didn't mean for it to happen but it did. I love you, Ginger."

Her heart skipped a beat as happiness soared through her. She'd never felt so loved. "I love you too, Foster. You are kind and giving. Hard and strong, yet gentle. I want you to be my husband. I'm tired of trying to deny my feelings for you. You've already been a good father to Molly."

He leaned down and touched her lips with his. The first kiss was light and fluttery, almost teasing. The second one he slanted his lips over hers, deepening the kiss. When he lifted up to look at her, he stroked her face. The third kiss would have knocked her down if she'd been standing. He put his tongue into her mouth, swirling it around until hers began to touch his. It was intoxicating; unlike anything she'd ever known.

How she wanted him. His tongue began to go in and out of her mouth, imitating how their union would be. Her breasts tightened and her nipples hardened in need, but they couldn't. She needed to heal inside. But once healed, she planned on making up for lost time.

"How long?" He asked his lips still on hers.

"How would I know?"

He pulled back and smiled at her. "I suppose we wait until you are no longer sore. Probably a few months."

"That sounds way too long. We'll figure it out together."

"I like that. Figuring it out together. Ginger Galway, will you marry me?"

"Of course I will." Her eyes misted. "I never thought I'd get married."

"Isn't it wonderful how life works?"

EPILOGUE

hree Months Later
"I feel completeness with you I never thought possible." Ginger looked down at her gold wedding band.

"I'm glad we didn't wait until spring. I wanted you every minute of every day and I wouldn't have been able to stand it much longer." Foster took her hand and kissed her palm. "I wanted to do it the right way and I'm so glad it didn't take as long as I thought for you to heal."

"And what a lucky break we had that thaw last month." She smiled and blushed when he winked at her. Foster took Molly from her arms while Patches looked on, purring.

"This little one has so much red hair she looks so much like you." Molly started to scream and her face, neck, and little fists turned red. "Oh my, she's got the temper to go with her hair."

She laughed. "That's a myth. Look at me. I'm never mad." She laughed when Foster didn't respond. "I'm that bad?"

He handed Molly back to her and took them both into his warm embrace. He smelled of the outdoors and horses. "There is nothing about you that is bad. It was my luckiest day when you decided to give birth in my barn. You make everything in life better. We'll make our own good memories to get rid of the bad."

She held onto him. He was her port in a very bad storm and he continued to be her rock. Theirs was a forever type of love. He gave as much love as he took, and he was never too tired to love her at night. "Finding your barn was a type of miracle. Now Christmas will always be a time for us to celebrate. It's the time we gave and received the greatest gift— love."

THE END

I'm so pleased you chose to read The Greatest Gift, and it's my sincere hope that you enjoyed the story. I would appreciate if you'd consider posting a review. This can help an author tremendously in obtaining a readership. My many thanks. ~ Kathleen

FREE DOWNLOAD

Love Before Midnight
By Kathleen Ball

Get you free copy of "Love Before Midnight"
When you sign up for the author's VIP mailing list

Get Started Here

LOVE SO DEEP

Samantha tried wrapping her scarf around her head, but the weight of the hardened ice kept dragging it down. The naysayers were right, winter came early—very early and with a vengeance. She stared at the pure white snow dotted with Ponderosa pines. Their branches bowed from the snowy burden. She'd doubted her survival the minute they banned her from the wagon train but as she walked away, she grew determined to survive. What a difference a few weeks made. As soon as the storm hit two days ago, her doubts returned.

She took a step and stumbled. The hem of her dress, caked with icy snow, made it hard going. With each step, her feet punched through the snow and sank. Her hands stung from the biting cold. Soon she wouldn't feel them anymore. She knew the signs of frostbite. Pushing herself upright she struggled on, one exhausting step at a time.

The wind howled and she wanted to cry at its sad song. She'd been on her own for two long weeks now. How she hated the pious women she'd traveled with. The death of her parents left her alone and a woman alone was not allowed on the wagon train. The married women believed she'd entice their husbands. The same women whose children she nursed when they were sick. The hypocrisy ate at her soul.

It was either marry Old Thomas or leave. She refused to marry, calling their bluff. Unfortunately, it wasn't a bluff. They threw her a sack of food and a canteen of water and left her behind.

Again, she fell face first into the snow. Struggling to rise, she shook her head. Maybe it'd be easier to just lay there and fall into a forever sleep. Her food was long ago eaten and her strength had held out surprisingly long, but now she wasn't sure it was worth the effort.

A horse nickered and she pushed herself up. Her heart skipped a beat in fright. On the horse sat a huge man covered in animal furs. His rifle lay across his lap.

"Get up," he said, his voice full of anger.

Samantha pushed and struggled until she stood. This was it. She just hoped her death would be painless. Putting her frigid hands on her hips, she brazenly studied him. His slate blue eyes were full of compassion. He held out his hand. She grasped it and he hauled her up in front of him.

"Let's get you warm." He opened his fur coat, pulled her against his warm body, and wrapped them both up. "Where are your people?"

"My people?"

"Yes, do you have a cabin here bouts? You shouldn't be out here alone. It's dangerous and in the snow it's easy to get lost."

Turning her head, she felt his warm breath against her cheek. His full beard brushed against her. "I'm on my own. I was hoping to find a town."

He didn't say anything else as he urged his steed forward. It was slow going in the snow but the horse seemed to know its way. Leaning back against his wide chest, her eyes closed.

She awoke with a start, not recognizing where she was. A fire danced in the massive stone fireplace, but beyond the firelight, it was dark. Pain shot through her hands and feet. It was expected with frostbite but she didn't know just how painful it was until now.

The cabin looked well built out of hand-hewed logs, and no wind came through the walls. It was tiny, but it probably suited the man who rescued her. Sitting up, she waited for her eyes to adjust to the semi-darkness. There was a big pile of furs in one corner, a table with two chairs, and a makeshift kitchen area. Wooden crates hung on the walls to serve as shelves and a roughly put together plank of wood with logs for legs held a few kitchen items and tools.

Above the pile of furs were pegs on which a few items of clothing hung. There was nothing fancy and nothing of convenience but it was warm. She was grateful to have shelter from the cold. The pain in her fingers was the worst and she dreaded looking at them. Slowly she pulled them out from under the covers and to her relief, they weren't blackened with severe frostbite.

The door opened and the man came in, a bundle of firewood in his arms. Kicking the door closed behind him, he then glanced in her direction. "So, you've decided to come back to this world, did ya?"

"How long was I asleep?" Her body tensed, not sure what he had in store for her.

He laid the wood next to the fireplace and threw a log on top of the fire. The flame blazed higher. "Only a day. You sure were hard to thaw, and I'm glad ya was out when I tended your hands and feet. Painful business it is."

"Thank you. They're still hurting. It was nice of you to tend to me. I was afraid I'd lose them. Actually, I figured I was going to die out there. I've never seen snow so early. I wonder how the others fared."

His dark brow rose. "Others? You said you were alone. Damn, I live up here to be away from folks, not to go rescue them." He took off his fur coat and sat down.

"I am, or was, alone. I got kicked off the wagon train and was left to fend for myself." Her voice contained the bitterness she couldn't hide.

"What in tarnation are you talking about? You must have done something pretty awful to be banned from the train."

"Of course."

His blue eyes widened and he ran his hand through his thick black hair. It hung past his shoulders and she wondered when was the last time he'd had it cut. "You might as well tell me. I'm not the type to judge."

"My parents died and they refused to let me travel with them alone. It was either marry old toothless Thomas or be thrown off the train. To my surprise they were serious and when I refused to marry Thomas they filled a sack with a meager amount of food, filled a canteen, and allowed me to take my coat and scarf with me." She paused as all the pain came rushing back. There hadn't even been time to mourn the passing of her dear mother and father.

"Miss, that's—"

"It's Samantha. Samantha Foley."

He nodded. "I'm Patrick McCrery. I have to say that's quite the yarn you're spinning."

She glanced away from his intense eyes. "I wish it was just a story."

"Well now, are ya sure ya weren't inviting the married men to look your way?"

A loud sigh was her reply. She'd thought the people on the wagon train were crazy, but now a stranger believed her capable of luring men. What was it about her that people assumed such an awful thing? "I thought you said no judgment."

"Aye, I did. How long ago did they put you out?"

"I'd say two weeks or so. I tried to follow by foot but they actually threw rocks at me to keep me away. As far as I'm concerned, they left me to die." A tear rolled down her face. "Ouch!" She tried to wipe it away.

"Don't cry. I hate crying. If ya want me to believe your story I will."

Her eyes narrowed. "Just what is it about me that screams whore to you?"

"You have pretty blonde hair, and a man could get lost in those big blue eyes of yours. I have to say you're nicely rounded in the right places. You don't seem very meek either."

"You think I should have married Thomas? He is shiftless and wanted me to be his worker, not a wife. It would have caused trouble since I had no inclination to lay with him. He surely would have beaten me for it too. So, maybe my predicament is my fault. I suppose I chose death over a life of sheer hell."

His face softened a bit but she could see the clouds of doubt in his eyes. "I bet you're hungry. I'll throw something together." There was an edge to his voice and it didn't invite any more conversation.

Lying back down, she figured she might as well try to regain her strength before she was put out again.

Patrick squatted before the fire, adding wild onion to his venison stew. It was his winter staple. He wasn't sure what to think. Her story, though far-fetched could be true. He'd heard of worse. Sometimes people on a wagon train turned on each other. Usually they just broke into smaller groups.

Who in their right mind would leave a woman behind? There was no way she was as innocent as she claimed.

Glancing over his shoulder, his eyes drank their fill of her. She was beautiful and while sleeping he could imagine her to be an angel, but he knew better. Most people weren't what they showed the world. No, many harbored secrets and prejudices. Samantha, he'd never known a woman with that name before. She was probably supposed to be a boy named Sam and her parents had chosen a female name.

Her honey blonde hair fanned out on the pillow. It'd been a long time since he'd seen a woman so fair. He went to town twice a year for supplies, other than that he lived a mostly solitary life. There were a few neighbors like him, who didn't like the closed-in feel of a town. He tried the town life for a bit but people were not a charitable lot. They never forgave his parents for their supposed sins.

Traps needed checking and he couldn't take the time to indulge himself in his musings. Grabbing his heavy coat, he glanced back at Samantha and went out into the cold. The frigid bite hit him full force and ducking his head against the wind, he made his way to the makeshift barn. His horse, Ahearn, was always ready and willing to go no matter what the weather. He more than earned his name, which meant Lord of Horses in Gaelic.

Leaving a woman to starve and freeze—what was the world coming to? He mounted his horse and off they went to make their way among the traps. He already had a good amount of the finest furs and it made him proud. Hard work always paid off.

They traveled from trap to trap and found nothing. Perhaps the woman brought some bad luck with her. His mother would have prayed over her and sent her on her way. He smiled. He missed his mother but at least he had many fond memories to get him through the hard times. The clouds were rolling into the mountains and they were in for more nasty weather. He turned Ahern toward home and off they went.

A set of small footprints caught his eye. He pulled up on the reins, stopping Ahern and jumped off. The prints looked to be a child's. Did Samantha leave a child behind? She didn't wear a ring. Was she married? He followed them for a while but they disappeared in the blowing snow. Still he searched but he came up empty. It was too damn cold for a child to survive out here but there was nothing else he could do.

Grabbing Ahearn's mane, he jumped onto his back and headed to the cabin. The wind picked up and the sky turned dark. He'd better hurry if he planned to make it home before the next storm blew in.

After getting Ahearn into the barn and dried off, he gave him extra hay and made sure there was water. Grabbing a rope, he fully intended to tie a line from the barn to the house in case there was a white out. More than one person had frozen to death just steps from their houses. A rustling sound in the hayloft caught his attention and he slowly made his way to the pile. A small black shoe stuck out but the rest hid beneath the hay.

"Achoo."

"Come on out, I know you're in there." His words were met with silence.

There was another sneeze and Patrick reached down and brushed the hay off a small child. A boy, a blond-haired, blue-eyed, boy.

"You'll freeze out here and die. Come to the house, your Ma's in there."

The boy's eyes widened but he remained silent. He stretched out both arms to Patrick and he grabbed him up into his arms. The poor child was skin and bone. What type of mother leaves her child out in the snow to die? Samantha had a lot of explaining to do.

"Let's get ya warm and dry. I even have food warming over the fire."

The boy nodded, put his head on Patrick's shoulder, and closed his eyes.

Samantha grabbed a tin plate and ladled some of the venison stew on it. Her stomach growled and her mouth watered. Her clothes were still damp so she grabbed one of Patrick's shirts and put it on. It was huge on her. She rolled up the sleeves and laughed. It practically hung to her feet.

He didn't seem to be one to smile often, but he hadn't tried to have his way with her either. Hoping for a peek outside, she opened the door, but the intense wind immediately pushed her back. It was a struggle to close the door. Hopefully Patrick wasn't too far away.

Her hands and feet still hurt, but not as much as the first time she woke. It was a good sign. Patrick must get supplies somewhere. The nearest town couldn't be too far away. As soon as the storm stopped, she'd be on her way. She hadn't quite figured out what she'd do once she got to town but she was sure there must be a kindly pastor and his wife to take her in for a bit.

Sitting at the table, she ate until she was full. It seemed to be forever since she'd had enough to eat. Supplies on the wagon train had been rationed and the hope for hunting quickly dimmed as the hunters returned day after day with no food.

She took her last bite when the door blew open with a

bang. Patrick stood in the doorway, carrying a child and glaring at her. "I found your child. I've heard about bad mothers but dang it ya are as cold hearted as they come. Why no mention of your son? You left him out there to die!"

Quickly standing, she backed up. "That is not my boy. I've never been married."

"Aha! So, the real skinny is coming to light. What happened the rest of the pious folks on the wagon train found out you have a bastard and threw ya out? Did you figure you'd be better off without proof of your sins?"

The back of her legs hit the bed and she immediately sat. "I don't know what you're talking about. That child needs tending. Bring him here."

"What's his name?" he asked as he laid him on the bed.

"How would I know?" She was glad her irritation showed in her voice. The mountain man was pure loco.

"You plan to play out your lies? Your heart must be iced over."

"He is not my child." She began to undress the boy and gasped. His bones were visible and he had more than a few bruises on him.

Patrick gaffed. "I wouldn't want to admit to the treatment of the boy either."

It was getting nearly impossible to keep her temper reined in. "Could you get me some warm water and a bit of muslin if you have it. I'd like to wash him off a bit."

He didn't say a word, he just did as she asked. He watched as she tenderly wiped the dirt away from the boy.

"From his thinness I'd say he'd been on his own for more than a few weeks. How old do you think he is?"

"He's puny enough to pass for three but I reckon he's at least four or so. He was smart enough to hide in my hay."

Samantha nodded. It didn't matter what Patrick thought,

she needed to tend to the boy. Someone out there was missing a child and they were probably heartbroken or dead. These mountains were unforgiving. She briefly wondered how the people on the wagon train were faring but dismissed them fast enough. They probably weren't wondering about her.

As soon as she washed the boy up, she tucked him into the massive bed. His eyes opened and he smiled. "Mommy?"

Before she could utter a word, Patrick sat on the edge of the bed. "You're fine now, lad. Your ma is right here. No more worries."

The boy nodded and instantly fell back to sleep.

Patrick stood and crossed his arms in front of him. His expression was thunderous. "Lies upon lies. If the wind wasn't howling like a banshee, I'd put you out. Children are innocents and no matter how they came into the world they deserve the same love as any other child."

She took a deep breath and slowly let it out. What was there to say? He didn't believe one word she said. Why the child called her mommy was a mystery but they did have the same coloring. His ma was probably blonde too. She'd lived a good, honest and respectable life. She obeyed her parents and tried to do what was right. Maybe it was all for naught. Patrick didn't care, he already judged her immoral.

"I hope his parents are alive somewhere and we can reunite them."

He laughed mockingly and shook his head. "Still insisting he's not yours huh? He did call you mommy. I think it's proof enough. You can stop with your untruths now."

She gave him a sad smile, walked by him, and grabbed one of the chairs. She put it closer to the fireplace and sat down. Maybe the storm would be over soon.

She had nerve, sticking to her story. How could she accept shelter from him when her child was out in the blizzard? Then there were the bruises on the child's body. He had to fight the urge to give her a bruise or two. He'd never hit a woman before and he didn't intend to start now, even if she did deserve it.

The cabin felt smaller, more closed in with her in it. She wasn't going to stay without working for her keep. "Can ya cook?"

She jerked her head and glanced at him. "Yes."

"What about keeping a place clean and the like?"

"I can do it all. Don't worry, I don't intend to sit around waiting for the snow to subside. I appreciate all you have done for me but I'll be lighting out as soon as possible."

"And the boy?"

"I don't even know his name. I know you don't believe me, but it's true. No, the boy will not be coming with me."

He grunted. "No sense arguing about it now. The snow will be there for months to come."

Her eyes widened and her throat dried. "Months?"

"Yes, months. You're in the high country. Once it snows it's pretty much going to keep snowing until spring." He briefly enjoyed her horrified expression, until he realized he was stuck with her. "You mentioned your parents died."

"My mother started to grow weaker and weaker and no matter what we tried, she died. It was only three weeks into the drive. My dad fell off his horse and broke his neck about two weeks ago. It was his turn to hunt and I drove the wagon. His horse showed up, dragging him." She closed her eyes. "It wasn't pleasant to see. We buried him and they banned me in the same day. I'll never get over losing my parents but being turned away hurt. I nursed many of the people on the train, especially the children. I helped to birth two, but in the end it didn't matter."

Her sadness tugged at his heart. "They banned the two of ya?"

"Two? Oh, you still think he's mine. No, they left me alone." She bristled.

"I see." He didn't see at all.

"Do you like living here alone? How far are you from town?"

"I enjoy my solitude. The town is a good two to three days away. I don't go in very often."

"Sounds lonely." Her voice grew soft.

"It can be but it's better than the alternative."

"The alternative?"

He started to reply but a cry from his bed drew his attention. They both went over to see the boy. He sat next to him and was surprised when he wrapped his arms around him and called him pa. Bewildered he turned and locked gazes with Samantha. She just shrugged.

"Do you know what your name is?"

"Yes, Sir, I'm Brian." He nodded hesitantly.

"I'm Patrick and, well, you know your ma."

Brian just nodded, his eyes widened as he stared at his mother. Then he smiled.

"How'd you end up outside all alone?" Patrick asked gently.

"I dunno. I don't think I know. How?" He raised his eyebrows waiting for an answer.

"Perhaps your ma knows."

"I don't think so. I don't think anyone knows."

"What's the last thing you remember?"

"I was sleeping in the back of a wagon. A man was takin' me to live with him. He said I'd be able to do a lot of work."

Patrick gave her a pointed look. "Doesn't sound like a good situation."

Brian smiled. "Here is better. Got any food?"

"I bet your ma could get you some food. I'd like some too."

Samantha stiffened but didn't say a word. She went to the pot hanging above the fire and stirred the stew before she ladled it onto two plates. She grabbed the two other forks he owned and brought them both food. "It's hot."

"Thank you."

She stared at him for a moment and then nodded. "You're welcome."

He sat on the edge of the bed and out of the corner of his eye, he saw Brian watching him and taking a bite when he did. He wanted to chuckle but thought it best not to. He wasn't sure what was going on but they'd be stuck with each other for a while and they needed to work things out. The first thing he needed to do was find Samantha's dress. The occasional peek at her shapely legs was starting to give him ideas. Ideas he had no business thinking. Maybe she would be interested in a relationship with him but he didn't want any children to come of it. It was better to keep his mind on other things.

"I'll go hunting tomorrow and see what I can find. For some reason my traps were all empty today. I don't rightly remember that ever happening before."

Brian hung his head. "Solomon stoled them."

His brow furrowed. "Solomon?"

"Yep, he's the man I belong to. He took all your animals and reset the traps. I must have fallen off the wagon."

"He has a wagon up here? It's sure to get stuck."

"We ain't from around here. We've been traveling and Solomon saw Ma get throwed away so he followed her but he said she was a tricky one and hard to find. He always took the animals. He likes the fur. Soon we were going to hunt for gold."

"Brian, I want ya to think hard before you answer my next question. Is she really your ma?"

Brian's hands shook but he looked Patrick straight in the eye. "Yes sir, she's my ma."

Continue Reading

ABOUT THE AUTHOR

Sexy Cowboys and the Women Who Love Them...
Finalist in the 2012 and 2015 RONE Awards.
Top Pick, Five Star Series from the Romance Review.
Kathleen Ball writes contemporary and historical western
romance with great emotion and
memorable characters. Her books are award winners and
have appeared on best sellers lists including: Amazon's Best
Seller's List, All Romance Ebooks, Bookstrand, Desert
Breeze Publishing and Secret Cravings Publishing Best
Sellers list. She is the recipient of eight Editor's Choice
Awards, and The Readers' Choice Award for Ryelee's
Cowboy.
Winner of the Lear diamond award Best Historical Novel-
Cinders' Bride
There's something about a cowboy

facebook.com/kathleenballwesternromance

twitter.com/kballauthor

instagram.com/author_kathleenball

So Many Roads to Choose

The Settlers

Greg

Juan

Scarlett

The Greatest Gift

Love So Deep

Luke's Fate

Whispered Love

Love Before Midnight

I'm Forever Yours

Finn's Fortune